Mai '22

Liebe Anne,
Lorna ist immer
  wieder eine Inspiration
für mich, was eigene
Bedürfnisse, Grenzen, Wünsche
und Kommunikation
  angeht.
Vielleicht ja auch
  für dich.

Jule

THE DRIVING FORCE OF FRIENDSHIP

The Wrong End of the Gun

LORNA RITCHIE
and
GODFREY SPENCER

Copyright © 2021 Lorna Ritchie and Godfrey Spencer.

All rights reserved. No part of this book may be used or reproduced by any means, graphic, electronic, or mechanical, including photocopying, recording, taping or by any information storage retrieval system without the written permission of the author except in the case of brief quotations embodied in critical articles and reviews.

Balboa Press books may be ordered through booksellers or by contacting:

Balboa Press
A Division of Hay House
1663 Liberty Drive
Bloomington, IN 47403
www.balboapress.com
844-682-1282

Because of the dynamic nature of the Internet, any web addresses or links contained in this book may have changed since publication and may no longer be valid. The views expressed in this work are solely those of the author and do not necessarily reflect the views of the publisher, and the publisher hereby disclaims any responsibility for them.

The author of this book does not dispense medical advice or prescribe the use of any technique as a form of treatment for physical, emotional, or medical problems without the advice of a physician, either directly or indirectly. The intent of the author is only to offer information of a general nature to help you in your quest for emotional and spiritual well-being. In the event you use any of the information in this book for yourself, which is your constitutional right, the author and the publisher assume no responsibility for your actions.

Any people depicted in stock imagery provided by Getty Images are models, and such images are being used for illustrative purposes only. Certain stock imagery © Getty Images.

Print information available on the last page.

ISBN: 978-1-9822-7188-6 (sc)
ISBN: 978-1-9822-7190-9 (hc)
ISBN: 978-1-9822-7189-3 (e)

Library of Congress Control Number: 2021914674

Balboa Press rev. date: 09/16/2021

In memory of Marshall B. Rosenberg, Klaus Karstädt and Marilyn Tresias, who passed from us in this world during this journey, but were with us in spirit every step of the way.

CONTENTS

All is Well ix
Foreword by Mary Mackenzie xi
Preface xv
Introduction xvii

Chapter 1   "Where the Hell Are We Going?" 1
Chapter 2   Wars, Home and Away 9
Chapter 3   Family Ties and Enemy Images 21
Chapter 4   An Exceptional Childhood 35
Chapter 5   On the Move 49
Chapter 6   Work, Rest and Play 65
Chapter 7   Introducing Marshall 87
Chapter 8   Empathic Interpretation 103
Chapter 9   The Intimacy of Conflict 115
Chapter 10 Needy Needs 133
Chapter 11 F'R'amily 151
Chapter 12 A Whirlwind Adventure 165
Chapter 13 Our Silence 177
Chapter 14 "Where In the World Do We Go Next?" ... 183

Epilogue 195
There is a Place 199
Acknowledgements 201
Resources 203

ALL IS WELL

By Cinde Borup and Beth Pederson

Come inside this forest deep and dark,
And walk along this path that winding through,
Gaze into each shadow that lies silent,
And waiting, and watching, watching you.

Though the forest seems so dark and still,
Unpenetrated by the smallest light,
Soon the path continues up the hill,
And opens under starry, starry night.

And all is well, and all is right,
All is well,
There is safety in the starry, starry night.

Untie the boat and slip out in the stream,
Into the mighty current deep and wide,
Up above a storm is gathering,
The shore is growing farther from my side.

Though the river runs so cold and fast,
Unchallenged by this tiny boat I row,
By and by the rapids are now past,
And there is comfort in the gentle river's flow.

And all is well, I'm safe and sound,
All is well,
There is peace upon my river homeward bound.

Come into this house so filled with light,
And walk among these people here today,
Everyone is sharing in this fight,
Everyone a traveller on the way.

We reach our destination even though
Every journey seems to hold some tears,
Look into ourselves to find the strength,
When we listen to our hearts we always hear:

That all is well, I'm safe and sound,
All is well,
There is peace upon my river homeward bound.

And all is well, and all is right,
All is well,
There is healing in the starry, starry night.

And all is well, and all is right,
All is well,
There is healing in the starry, starry night.

FOREWORD BY MARY MACKENZIE

In their book, Lorna and Godfrey lead us into a thoughtful and intimate journey into their 15-year friendship. Along the way, they drive through Europe (a few times!) as they dive into one gripping topic after another on their long road trips. Things like war, humanity, empathy, parenting, domestic violence, the toxicity of obligations and how confusing it can be to navigate a desire for trust, authenticity and choice, and ultimately the challenge of shifting from a mentor/mentee relationship to friendship, are all up for discussion.

Sometimes the stories have so much grit to them I would feel my eyebrows raise up in consternation. What was especially compelling, though, was reading how Lorna and Godfrey grappled with these meaty issues. And, I confess, there was a time or two when I was even tempted to call Lorna or Godfrey and say, "What? Really?"

I could have done that because I have been a colleague for 15 years or so. Still, calling them seemed like the easy way out. Even more compelling for me was to read about their conversations and take in the information with my own filters and life experiences, and decide how I felt about them.

I learned things about myself in the process. I grew in my own understanding of who I have been and who I am now as a friend, wife, sister, daughter, stepmother, grandmother, and boss. I grew to appreciate the relationships that I experience as equal in power - and I became keenly aware of those that aren't. I stretched my thinking and re-examined my biases.

I write this with some humility because I have been teaching Nonviolent Communication for over 21 years, and I consider myself somewhat of an expert on relationships and in relating to others. Yet, if my last 21 years have taught me anything it is that the very act of being in relationship with others calls us to expand and stretch, and there are no absolutes. Lorna and Godfrey reminded me of this often.

Initially, I thought their book was a memoir, but I soon learned that it is much more than that. I realised that they were taking me on a journey and, as I followed along, I began to notice subtle shifts in their relationship as they progressed from Godfrey as Lorna's teacher, to Godfrey and Lorna as equal friends. I was touched to read about the times when there was friction between them because I could so relate to those moments, and I was delighted when they found their way back to connection.

The progression of their relationship is summed up for me in two quotes from their book:

"… 'Ubuntu' or shared humanity… I am because of who we all are,' which speaks to the fact that we are all connected and that one can only grow and progress through the growth and progression of other." (chapter 7)

"We have to work collectively, with an acute sense of 'us and we.'" (chapter 14)

If you're like me, you will find *The Driving Force of Friendship* expands your own understanding of friendship, forces you to look deeper into intimate topics that are seldom discussed, and do a bit of your own inner healing. And, don't be a bit surprised if you laugh out loud as they argue about whether to take a right or left on the road! An argument I can so relate to!

A dear friend of mine of 25 years died recently. She was my mentor in the early years of our friendship. We spent the last few years of her life shifting the dynamics of our relationship from mentor/friend to friend/friend and we didn't complete the process. I felt bereft, deeply sad and confused about what happened in our friendship that didn't allow for true closure before she died.

Then I read *The Driving Force of Friendship* by Lorna Ritchie and Godfrey Spencer… and I understood…

Mary Mackenzie, M.A., Co-founder, NVC Academy
Author, Peaceful Living: Daily Meditations for Living with Love, Healing and Compassion
Certified Trainer of Nonviolent Communication

PREFACE

I have many stories; a veritable library of lived experience that I began filing away more than seventy years ago as a boy living in post-war Britain. But it was my dear friend and colleague Lorna Ritchie's idea to commit them to paper in a book about our friendship.

Lorna and I have spent many hours together driving through Europe to attend meetings, conferences and milestone moments related to our work as trainers in Nonviolent Communication (NVC), she at the wheel and me as her grateful passenger telling tales to entertain her. During those times, we delved into the complexities of our upbringings, our hopes, our dreams, our points of view on topics ranging from the precise meaning of NVC founder Marshall Rosenberg's concept of 'street giraffe' – I won't enlighten you here! – to the impact of the Black Lives Matter and Extinction Rebellion movements.

What started as Lorna's offer of a lift to a professional event has since blossomed into a beautiful connection between two people of different ages, genders, social backgrounds and outlooks. What unites us is a desire to see a better, fairer world where people learn to communicate and reach out to each other using NVC. We both long for a world of peace, empathy and compassion, and lots of fun.

The fruit of our friendship and our conversations is this book. I hope you enjoy reading it as much as I have enjoyed the times recounted in it.

Godfrey Spencer, certified NVC trainer (CNVC),
consultant and mediator.

INTRODUCTION

Our first title for this book, "The Wrong End of the Gun," came to us early on. After hearing Godfrey recount an incident in Turkey involving a shepherd, a tour guide and a twelve-bore shotgun, I commented, "Well, he was at the wrong end of that gun." Godfrey's retort was swift. "There is no right end."

Our stories, recounted in this book, prove that statement to be true. In these chapters, you'll glimpse the impact the concept of Nonviolent Communication, domestic violence, wars and love have had on mine and Godfrey's lives wrapped in a unique travelogue and a culinary tour through Europe. But more than that, this book is, in essence, the story of an unlikely friendship. If friendship is the key to some of life's treasures, then empathy is the lock that opens the door to that rich human experience, always allowing us opportunities to come closer together rather than remain separate.

I hope this is a valuable book for those who have never heard of NVC - and also those who practice it. But mostly, it's our story of life, love and personal connection.

Lorna Ritchie, certified NVC trainer (CNVC),
mediator, facilitator, business coach.

CHAPTER 1

"WHERE THE HELL ARE WE GOING?"

On that sunny weekday morning, the Boulevard Périphérique, the concrete tangle of lanes and junctions that encircles the beautiful French capital, was choked with vehicles. Traffic raced left and right. A red van cut in front of my little Citroen Pluriel, and I jumped on the brakes. Ahead, the motorway split off in two directions. I gripped the wheel. The calm female voice of the satnav instructed us to remain in the left lane. I glanced at my passenger, an acquaintance I'd agreed to give a lift to the south of France, and in that moment, realised he was panicking.

"No!" Godfrey screamed, waving his hand. "Stay right!"

Madame SatNav insisted: "Stay in the left lane and keep left."

An enormous interchange loomed ahead.

"Take the right-hand lane," Godfrey's face turned red. "Do it! Ignore her. Go right! I've done this before. She's wrong!"

I switched into the adjacent lane and turned down Madame SatNav before she could tell me off. Ahead, about three hundred metres on, the line of vehicles in front of us ground to a halt. Traffic jam. I turned to look at my navigator, a seventy-two-year-old Englishman with pale skin and even whiter hair, breathing heavily. He grunted.

We both took a deep breath and sat in silence as the car engine hummed.

"I'm not saying anything," I said quietly, swallowing my sarcasm.

We looked at each other and started sniggering like children before bursting into laughter at the ridiculousness of our situation.

I had first met Godfrey Spencer more than a decade earlier in 2004 at an International Intensive Training (IIT) course in Nonviolent Communication (NVC) held in Budapest and hosted for Marshall Rosenberg, the founder of the life-changing communication process.

Marshall had been sharing NVC worldwide as a counsellor, mediator and teacher. I attended as a participant, while Godfrey was one of six trainers working with Marshall. The event was packed with around fifty eager attendees speaking fourteen different languages. In NVC, words and how they are spoken, received, and understood, are critical. Teaching sessions were split into 'whispering groups' of people who shared the same mother tongue and a translator who interpreted for them in hushed tones. When not teaching himself, Godfrey also acted as an interpreter. We hit it off immediately. We shared the same sense of silly dry British humour. But it wouldn't be until we embarked on this car journey in 2012, the first of many across Europe, that we would become firm friends.

My friendship with Godfrey is the closest platonic relationship I've had with an older man.

In the car, I stared straight ahead at the tail lights blinking as the tower blocks lining the Périphérique loomed over us. We had at least eight hours of driving ahead of us before we reached Montolieu, a beautiful hillside village not far from Toulouse famous for its bookshops and creative community and the home of the Peace Factory, the venue for the first European Intensive Course (EIC) in NVC.

Godfrey had heard that I'd be driving to the event from Berlin, my chosen home since 1983. My route took me via Brussels, where I would visit an old friend. Godfrey lived there at the time with one of his daughters and asked me for a lift. I love to drive. Godfrey, I was to learn, is nervous at the wheel.

Attendees of NVC events are encouraged to coordinate their travel, and I'd seen folk on social media offering lifts or a couch to sleep on en route. I was hesitant to put myself forward, feeling a little shy of driving with a stranger. But, realising Godfrey was living in Brussels, directly on my route, I emailed, suggesting we have a coffee before he made his way to Montolieu. He was to be part of the trainer team and I was a participant. When he suggested we drive together I was tickled pink. Remembering his quick wit from the IIT, I was confident it would be a cheerful journey. Secretly I felt honoured he asked. There is always an element of reverence and privilege having extra time with 'the teacher'. And having lived as an ex-pat in Germany for so long, I missed chatting with another Brit, reminiscing as you do, nostalgic for the homeland. There are some things only another British ex-pat will understand: the excitement of finding Digestive Biscuits or Branston Pickle in a store, British comedy shows, the desire to queue, the deep sense of relief when met with politeness and customer care, and the need to understate or poke fun at everything. This shared history created an unspoken sense of ease and belonging between us.

It was late in the evening when I arrived at Godfrey's daughter's townhouse in the Belgian capital. As I stood in the slender entrance hall with impossibly high ceilings, any image I'd held of Godfrey as a patriarchal authority figure dissipated. I was brought up to respect my elders and Godfrey's age and experience triggered a humility in me that had led me to make assumptions. His kindness and generous nature had always been apparent, but his general demeanour was one of privilege, which I had come to know so well as I straddled the class system in England in the seventies. Instead of hierarchy, I entered an atmosphere in this home akin to shared student accommodation. He and his daughter made me feel immediately at home. I was guided to his granddaughter's bedroom and fell into a deep sleep surrounded by teenage artwork, bright linens, colourfully hand-painted walls and shoes strewn over the floor. We headed out the next morning at seven hoping to miss the rush hour traffic.

As we turned off the Paris ring road to head south, passing the exit to the airport, our course correction behind us, the number of vehicles thinned out on the dual carriageway and the concrete was replaced by grass verges, trees and shrubs. I let my shoulders drop after the tension of the traffic snarl and began to relax into a more convivial atmosphere. We both heaved sighs of relief and I turned on some gentle summer music.

Godfrey turned to me. "I'm seriously happy Lorna that you are driving me. About a year or so ago I had a really scary experience. It was late, around eleven, and I was driving home to Brussels from the Ardennes. I was tired and almost there when a car overtook me on the hard shoulder, right between me and the safety rail, then cut in front of me. I pulled across and lost focus and when I came to, the car was rushing over wet grass and up a bank, towards a tall lamppost. It gently came to a halt and the driver's side door fell open when I got out on the sloping verge and I had no idea where I was. I didn't even know what country I was in. It was pitch black, but I spotted a sign and realised it was for my exit and breathed a sigh of relief. I phoned my wife who phoned the police, who arrived quickly, with big flashing lights and a huge breakdown truck with a crane. They placed a belt under the roof of the car and hoisted it up."

I glanced at my companion whose face was stricken with fear recalling the incident.

"So, what had happened?"

"I have no idea. I take naps in the day when I get tired so I thought perhaps I'd fallen asleep. But when I saw my oncologist later the same week, he said he thought I'd had something called an absence seizure and that would explain my disorientation. He suggested a CT scan of my brain, which revealed an anomaly, little bubbles at the spot where an artery and some veins join. He wanted to operate, but such a procedure would be risky because the problem was located so deep in the tissue. I sought a second opinion, which took about a year to get, and have now decided just to live with it, especially as it has been there all my life. It's no more a problem now than it's been at any other time."

I was touched that Godfrey shared such a vulnerable experience and had been holding my breath while he spoke. I was going to get used to his many stories of shock and horror but for that moment, I envisaged briefly a scenario in which I would have to give him CPR. I blinked the image away.

Godfrey continued: "That said, when I think about dying, I think I'll have a sudden death, because if any of those bubbles burst, I won't last long."

I kept my eyes on the road. "That's a cheery thought!"

"Well, we all have to die some time, and I'm over seventy! But I may still retire in forty years' time!"

We both chuckled.

"In fact, I'm no more concerned about death now I have this diagnosis than I was before. It has helped me to realise that death is just a part of life. I feel much calmer about its approach, whether it's in two minutes or several years, and I'm pleased about that."

I felt relieved and was enjoying this British habit of making light of any difficulty or fear. I wondered if I should tell him of my daily practice of imagining today to be my last day, which I use in order to focus myself on my priorities, to be totally present in the moment. I smiled, saving that for later. We had a long journey ahead. Instead, I picked up the thread he had given me.

"So, because of this diagnosis you don't like to drive?"

"No, not really. I worry, like everyone else, that I will have an accident and be killed or kill someone else. I particularly don't want to kill anyone else. So, I've drawn back on my driving. I tend to take planes and trains instead. That you're driving me to this course in Montolieu is a great gift to me. I don't have to worry at all, because if I am killed, I'm the passenger rather than the driver, and nobody else dies because of me."

"Good grief!" I pretended to be shocked for dramatic effect, but actually I enjoyed his indifference. "That's a relaxing thought! The blood will be on my hands." I thought of his reaction to Madame SatNav earlier and softened my voice. "But you are still worried about being in a car?"

"Taking a wrong turn is a really sensitive issue, because I think about the danger of missing a particular junction and then about the time wasted driving the wrong way." Godfrey took a slightly self-mocking tone. "When I drive myself, I override any mechanical system like a GPS because I'm certain that I know the way!"

My passenger was turning out to be a fascinating travelling companion, complex, deeply sincere, authentic, an open book. I was enjoying Godfrey's company, his subtle habit of self-deprecation. I wondered if that was something about being British and not allowing yourself to seem too self-important or self-satisfied. I felt confident enough to be honest about my feelings regarding his burst of anger on the Boulevard Périphérique.

"Your reaction back in Paris did surprise me actually."

Godfrey considered my statement. "When I think I'm right, any notion of your needs goes out of the window and I just want you to do as I say." He sighed. "I know this conflicts with the NVC concept that nothing is right or wrong. But I would feel the same about you tying your shoelaces. If you tie them in a way that I think is wrong, I will tell you so. And if they come undone, I will say 'I told you so'."

I laughed out loud. Here was an NVC trainer, who spent most of his days imparting the wisdom that it is important to avoid judgements in our thinking and communication, getting real, showing me another very private side of himself. His self-confidence to do so, I found heart-warming, especially because he served it with subtle self-criticism.

Godfrey continued to explain that there is in fact a way to knot a shoelace that will stay tied all day unless the strings are pulled gently at the same time. "Which means it's the easiest knot to untie," he stated. "Anyway, I'm trying to explain why I insisted the GPS was wrong." He paused. "But then you actually did what I said."

"Well, the GPS wasn't going to insult me if I took a wrong turn."

I couldn't stop myself wanting to rub it in a little. Then he took an empathic guess at my needs.

"So, you feared my reaction more than the reaction of the GPS? You just wanted to have some peace and harmony?"

I hadn't been scared when Godfrey had shouted. My respect for him as my passenger, my elder and also being knowledgeable about the roads around Paris had compelled me to do as he said. But actually his advice had made things worse.

The car sped along the main road cutting through flat French countryside. I rolled my eyes and muttered, "Damned empathy!"

We started to chuckle again, two trainers, counsellors and mediators trained in the art of understanding another's needs and feelings, riding along together. I knew then our journey was going to be a unique experience.

"Entertain me, Godfrey. Tell me about your life."

CHAPTER 2

WARS, HOME AND AWAY

Landing at London Heathrow always feels like coming home to me, even though I have been living in Berlin for more than three decades. This time, I was on my way to a ten-day NVC retreat in Wales focused on living compassionately. After I picked up the hire car, I headed out onto the M4 motorway, still getting accustomed to driving on the left-hand side, the tiny lanes in the towns, and noticing the beautiful autumn hues of the hedgerows.

Beyond the M25, the motorway that circles London, I passed the urban sprawl of Slough on my right and Windsor to my left, where the Queen sometimes resides in one of her castles. In under an hour, I had arrived at Reading train station. I spotted Godfrey waiting for me, searching for something in his backpack. It took several minutes for him to load his bags into the car and I was happy to wait. I lit a cigarette while he checked and double-checked for his keys, phone and bits and bobs. This was his routine. He had done the same a few months before, when I had dropped him off at Toulouse airport after the training in Montolieu.

As I leaned against the car, I felt a sense of ease and familiarity. I wondered what our journey held. And I also wondered what the retreat would be like with both of us attending as participants on equal terms. I found Godfrey's willingness to attend inspiring. He was still eager to expand and learn, to take on the role of student, even after all his years as a trainer.

On the road, instead of continuing directly west, we curved north toward the patchwork of farmland and woods covering the Chiltern Hills. The Oxfordshire landscape had changed little since I spent my childhood there in the seventies. The gentle rolling hills, farmlands, pastures, woodlands and valleys took me back to Sunday afternoon outings with my parents. As the daughter of Irish immigrants, I grew up an only child, although my parents had other children between them with their previous spouses, who I wouldn't learn about until years later.

I remembered those childhood days with mixed feelings.

Seeing a sign for Blackbird Leys, a vast council estate of close to three thousand flats where we moved when I was five, I held my breath and accelerated, although I felt a prick of curiosity about how it might have changed. In 1970, it was already a pretty rough place, housing the population overspill from the city. We were largely immigrant residents. Many of the men worked in the nearby Leyland car factory, as did my father. He was a Catholic, my mother a Protestant. They had both fled 'The Troubles' in Northern Ireland in 1965. Diverse in race and culture, the working-class community in Blackbird Leys was notorious for its social tensions, teenage pregnancies and single-parent families. Despite the poverty, or maybe as a result of it, there was a great sense of community and sharing, borrowing, lending, helping each other out, all values my parents held. Crime, vandalism, domestic violence, life as a foreigner in England were also common realities that all the kids in my little gang had to learn to deal with. We were a totally mixed bunch, ranging from five to thirteen years of age, each looking out for the other if need be, but powerless in the face of adult abuse.

I looked at my companion, wondering whether to share my history. I shook my head, no, not today. I felt shy about touching on such vulnerable memories. And, in any case, it was not the deal I'd struck with Godfrey: I drive, he entertains me with stories from his remarkable life.

"What's your earliest memory Godfrey?"

He answered quickly. "Of life in Mayfield, Sussex, and the German V2 bombs flying over our heads. As long as you could see a little red tennis ball of flame soaring through the sky then all was well. If you couldn't, that meant the missile's fuel had finally run out and it was about to drop on its target. As you craned to watch it pass, you hoped that spark would remain in sight and travel on for a long time." His voice quavered. "Two V2s landed very near our house, one in the field where the pony grazed, and another on a cinema filled with one hundred and twenty people. They all died. Violence was very much in the air that I breathed as a child. Guns have loomed very large, whether it was during the war or in later life. It seems I've seen a lot of people maimed and killed by violence, bombs and guns."

I nodded, listening.

"And it has affected me very deeply."

Of that I was certain. It must have been traumatic to be afraid of the world outside and the danger there. It occurred to me that the damage and coping skills developed by children who feared violence outside compared to children who were terrified of violence inside the home might be different. Our conversation turned to examine this, both relieved, it seemed, to engage in an intellectual discussion rather than stay with the images circling in our heads.

Skirting Oxford's historic city centre, we continued on the A40 to Burford, a small market town on the banks of the River Windrush in the Cotswold Hills. As we searched for somewhere to eat on the high street of stone buildings, some dating back to the medieval period, we paused to cross the road. I slipped my arm through Godfrey's to hold onto him. He had a tendency to rush on ahead when he was on a mission. Looking down at the pavement as we waited for a car to park, Godfrey returned to the theme that was clearly still churning in his mind.

"One day, when I was about four, I was walking on a very high pavement and a column of Bren Gun Carriers trundled along up the road toward us. With its armour plating, tracks and a machine gun poking out the front, they look like tanks. The drivers inside must have received orders to all turn at the same time and the carrier passing in front of me swung around ripping out about three feet of the pavement from underneath my feet. If that tank had moved another three feet, I would have been swept out of this life. That was when the war entered my life. It was a taste of what my father was experiencing miles away in Iceland. When he was posted there to act as liaison officer between the Royal Air Force and the US Air Force, I didn't know if he would return."

Standing arm-in-arm with him in the street, feeling him tremble as he recounted this story, I listened intently. I felt honoured and humbled to hear him talk about the Second World War. No one in my childhood spoke of it. It wasn't until I moved to Germany that I heard people talk openly about what they went through in their communities, and even then, they rarely shared personal stories. I felt I was there with him, reliving the scenes.

We stepped off the pavement. Godfrey continued: "I remember one morning my grandmother took me to kindergarten. I watched her turn to go home before I slipped off to the train station and spent the morning sitting on the platform watching the engines come and go. I must have imagined that maybe my father would arrive home on one of the trains. Of course, he didn't, but I stayed there. At around noon, the station master shooed me away. I walked back towards school and caught sight of my grandmother turning on her heel and heading home without me." Godfrey paused. "This is a very tender memory. I caught up with her and told her where I'd been." I squeezed his arm. "She didn't tell me off. She just told me that she had been worried because she didn't know where I was and because no one had seen me all morning."

"How gentle of her to react like that. My Irish mother would have dealt a swift clip to the ear."

We reached the other side of the road.

"The war left me with memories of obliteration and the realisation that what is here today might not be here tomorrow."

With that thought still ringing in our heads, we settled in the cosy lounge of the Bay Tree Hotel warmed by a log fire, and ordered tea and cakes. Neither of us was in a rush. It struck me that conversations between Godfrey and me quickly reached an emotional intensity and connection, in stark contrast to the distance created by the emotional intensity inflicted on us growing up. I was beginning to realise we both shared childhoods permeated with fear, violence and insecurity and that we had both learned to hold a lot of that inside. There had been no space for a child to have an outburst.

Godfrey and I never dallied in small talk, thanks in part to our NVC training, which enabled us to get quickly to the core of what was being said. I think we both felt that life was too short to waste time on chit-chat. Godfrey had been reminded of this most recently during his car crash in the Ardennes. And I had been in Sri Lanka the winter of 2004, just after we first met, when the tsunami hit, drowning tens of thousands of people. Sitting on the comfy sofas in the low-ceilinged room, we knew that we would soon be among a large group of people all learning and living in the spirit of Nonviolent Communication and probably wouldn't have many quiet moments of connection with each other during the upcoming retreat.

"What happened to you after the war?" I sipped my tea.

"My father got a job in Thorington in Suffolk, where a tea planter and importer was looking for a farm manager, and we all went with him. Initially he didn't work on the farm but did some market gardening, which was an absolute failure, because the soil was very light and sandy. One year you got carrots that weighed a kilo each and the next year you got tiny finger-sized vegetables that you couldn't sell either. When we finally moved to the farmhouse on the property, we had everything we needed and were more comfortable; wheat to make flour, eggs, kitchen garden, greenhouse. Unlike elsewhere, we had no worries about food. As a child, I was very interested in agriculture and used to chat to the farm workers a lot. I picked up the local dialect, so I obviously had an ear for languages at an early age. It was also with them that I had my first and last cigarette at the age of seven."

I smiled and wished my first had been my last, having smoked on and off for thirty-five years.

"Was your life more settled?"

"There were no more bombs, but there were guns. The government supplied farms with ammunition to shoot rabbits and pigeons to keep their populations in check. It sounds quite innocent, but it got you used to killing. I must have been about ten when I was allowed to use my father's twelve-bore, and he realised that I was a good shot. I was often posted between our little wood and one of the fields to shoot wildlife. We didn't kill them for food, but to protect the crops. One time, a boy in our village climbed a tree with a .22 rifle, but he didn't break the gun before he scrambled down and it went off accidentally. The bullet entered straight into his hip. On a different occasion, a neighbour gave his son a rifle and on the very same day the son killed his brother by accident."

His stories made me think of the old black and white films I watched as a child sitting beside my mother as she smiled, remembering when she first saw them at the cinema and with whom. In my childlike reflection, Godfrey could have been Mickey Rooney or Spencer Tracey. I had a romantic, sentimental idea of growing up on a farm with siblings, loving parents, enough food, being self-sufficient. I did not enjoy Godfrey's stories about people and animals getting shot, of which he had many. But it made me grateful that my parents had not had access to firearms, or theirs would have been a short relationship indeed.

"But you never got hurt?"

"When I was nine, I was up a tree and my older brother Hugh shot at me with his air-gun and the pellet cut into the flesh between two ribs. It didn't do any lasting physical damage, although I could have been paralysed if the pellet had entered my spine. Another time, Hugh had a twelve-bore and his plan was to shoot several starlings with one shot because they were eating the pig food. He saw seven of them sitting in a line on a wall and he was about to fire when I must have appeared and he turned the gun round and shot at the ground just in front of my foot. The shot made a crater in the concrete. He knew what he was doing with a gun, but it was a very, very scary thing to do."

"Jeez!" I shook my head.

"I adored Hugh, who was five years older than me, but I was also afraid of him. He pointed his airgun at my favourite cat and the little lead pellet lodged in his tail and stayed there. You could feel it when you stroked him."

"Was he always mean to you?"

"Hugh would twist and bend my little fingers and practise 'being a German on an Englishman'. Torture was part of the game of war. I didn't learn to defend myself; I just let it happen, because he was bigger than me and I chose not to defend myself. See my fingers are misshapen to this day." Godfrey held out his hands, lined and crinkled and dappled with age spots and with slightly bent pinky fingers. "There was another boy from London who stayed with us and he chased me round the farm with a wooden mallet, encouraged by my father. Although he was younger and smaller than me, I again didn't defend myself, because I didn't want to hurt him – or be scolded for hurting him."

Godfrey paid the bill and we wandered back to the car.

Sitting behind the wheel, I turned on the ignition and checked the GPS for directions. I glanced at Godfrey and noticed tears welling up in his eyes.

"Godfrey?"

"As a child, my big worries were my father's verbal abuse and mother's strictness. Father must have had a big voice because a neighbour a mile away could hear him shout. It was like being beaten on the eardrums when he screamed at you. I was the only one of us seven children who stuck around when he let rip. I know now that

I did that because I sensed he needed help in his moment of anger and I didn't want to walk out on him. I believe he was very grateful for that. He expressed it in his own way by telling people I was going to become a farmer, just like him. I understood this to mean I was worthy to follow in his footsteps."

"Was he physically violent toward you?"

"Just once. I went into my parents' room to get something and discovered him standing there in just his underpants. He had a belt in his hand and gave me one wallop. He was humiliated. In a way, I look back at those years and it was as if another kind of war was going on."

A deep twang of recognition resounded in me. My parents always said they left Northern Ireland because of 'The Troubles', the ongoing civil war between Catholics and Protestants that split communities and killed thousands. As a child, I believed a rather romantic notion that because they came from warring sides and weren't able to be together in their home town, they had been forced to settle in England. While that external war continued, my parents' relationship was strained from the start. Their connection was unstable, put under further pressure by the move to England and marred by poverty and violence.

When my father shouted it had never occurred to me that it was a cry for help. My instinct was either run like hell or pretend all was well, to pacify or distract alarmed outsiders, like the social workers who were present in my life from my earliest years, some of which I spent in foster families. Of them I have fond if sketchy memories.

I instantly recognised the signs of an argument brewing. My father would come home drunk, which riled my mother. He lost his temper and smashed up the kitchen, then her.

My earliest memories include screams, blows, shouting and the crockery breaking. Although, they never touched me. It would be me that accompanied my mother to the doctor's the next day, while my father disappeared for weeks, sometimes months and a peace would descend on our flat. Empty food cupboards were the price of that tranquillity. And then, I'd return home from school one day and find them together in the kitchen, where they would announce, sheepishly, that he was moving back in.

I turned my attention to Godfrey in the passenger seat and felt bewilderment at the ease with which he could speak of his experience of war and of domestic abuse. Short, coherent, detailed and often touching or funny stories, he was seemingly comfortable talking about his past albeit interspersed with frequent tears. I listened, empathised, hinted at some common ground and shared the odd detail to indicate I understood his experiences, but I did not share my story with him.

With my hands on the wheel, I thought to myself, not just yet.

I wondered, was it that my background was just too complex to delve into, or was I still traumatised, even after all the healing work I'd done over the years in Berlin? I certainly didn't cry as openly as Godfrey did. What was different in his story to mine? I wanted to hear more.

"Where was there love and support for you in your family?"

"My grandmother was a source of support. She lived about five miles away. She was a very wise woman, very kind. She talked to me about her life, about my grandfather whom I never knew, about her worries regarding my mother. When I went to primary school in Southwold, I lived with her for a while, which was quite a relief. But there was fear there too. My grandmother was a Catholic convert and a great proponent of the principle of right and wrong. If you didn't tell the truth or took something that wasn't yours, you were in great trouble and would go to hell. Her god presided over everything and was a god of retribution. Although neither she nor my parents went in much for physical punishment, it was clear that penance was coming in the afterlife, that God would get you in the end. I lived with the fear of that god for many years."

Remaining silent I pondered the role of religion in my upbringing. We didn't have a bible in the house, I never saw my parents pray and the only guilt I knew was in the realisation that with my birth, my parents were forced to leave Northern Ireland. I was spared religious indoctrination, except when they expressed disdain for 'the other side'. I am so glad to have found my own different kind of spirituality as an adult.

As we left Burford behind and headed into the Cotswolds, still lost in thought, I gazed over at my travelling partner. I could see the love he held for his grandmother still there. I wanted to hear more about her.

CHAPTER 3

FAMILY TIES AND ENEMY IMAGES

Taking smaller A-roads to avoid the motorway, we drove through the gentle rolling hills of the Cotswolds and on towards Bristol, then on to the M48 crossing the River Severn on the famous suspension bridge from Aust to Chepstow, and entered into Wales. The Wye Valley, with its limestone gorge scenery, river cliffs, expanses of woodland, meanders, floodplains, farms and cottages dotted across the landscape cut through by a glittering river, is an area of outstanding natural beauty. Our destination was a nineteenth century country manor house in a tiny village that boasted its own castle, built almost a thousand years ago as a defence against English invaders. As the car wound through the valley, Godfrey continued to tell me about his mother's mother Dorothy.

"You know Lorna, my grandmother was the first person I did a role-play with – at her behest."

I smiled. Role-playing is a key NVC technique that helps you see a situation through another person's eyes.

Godfrey's face softened at the memory. "When I was an undergraduate at Cambridge, my grandmother moved there so I could live with her and I took my meals at her kitchen table next to the window." He gave me a cheeky grin. "The curtains were there, of course, for me to wipe my hands on." We chuckled. "One day, my grandmother said to me, 'I don't like it when you wipe your hands on the curtains because they are difficult to clean. I have to unhook them, take them down, wash, iron and hang them up again.'

I listened, feeling guilty and unsettled. To prove her point, my grandmother suggested we swap places. She sat opposite me in my university gown, my square mortar board perched on her head. I found a piece of furry grey material and fastened it in place on my head with a woolly hat, threw a shawl around my shoulders and perched her spectacles half way down my nose.

Adopting her tone of voice, I spoke first. 'You really can't go on wiping your hands on my curtains, it's so disgusting.'

She responded as me: 'I feel really awkward now because I don't really want to wipe my hands on your curtains. But it's the easiest thing because they're near.'"

Godfrey and I giggled. The green hills passed along outside our little bubble of intimacy in the car.

"It was a wonderful moment, that ability to see another's perspective. I regret that I didn't continue to do role-plays in my private relationships from that day on. Once you step into the other person's shoes, it's just so easy to see their point of view. Then the problem is quickly solved."

I nodded. "Sounds like she was having fun playing your role, did you enjoy it?"

"Oh, we both laughed our heads off! She took a photograph of that moment, which I still have. I'm infinitely grateful to my grandmother for being who she was, because she was so affectionate and open, so understanding! When I was being badly treated by my elder brother who called me 'Granny's super-cuddled-blub-baby', she just dismissed it. She had no criticism for me, but no pity either. She just said, 'Godfrey, I love you for who you are and I also love your brother for who he is, and he's in a lot of pain.'"

I thought about the relationship between the two brothers. For most of my childhood, I had believed that I was an only child. I longed for siblings, only to discover when I was ten, that I had fifteen of them. Back in their hometown in Northern Ireland, my parents had been neighbours, each married to their respective spouses. My father, Frank, had ten children, and my mother four. I learned much later that my mother, Jean, had given up a child for adoption before she married her husband, making it five. I was born in 1965, the result of Frank and Jean's extramarital affair. My arrival coincided with a change in the political climate in Northern Ireland, the beginning of 'The Troubles' and the emergence of several sectarian paramilitary groups, unionists and nationalists, who engaged in armed actions. Thousands of Irish immigrants settling in England in the sixties were looking for work or seeking distance from that political conflict. My parents' move to Oxford was an attempt to leave behind the shame, heartbreak and attendant danger they had caused for themselves and their families.

They tweaked the truth of their lives in Ireland to ease the assimilation into their new community and possibly, I believe, to quieten their own emotional distress. The official story I was told was that my mother was a widow and I called my biological father 'Uncle Frank'. She spoke of him as her 'common-law husband'. I truly believed that her supposedly late husband was my father and had died after my birth. His name was on my birth certificate. I imagined him to be a very kind and gentle man and dreamed of a life with happy, caring, stable parents and loving siblings, never imagining they could be mean like Godfrey's brother.

Listening to him speak of his grandmother reminded me of the gentle, caring wisdom I had dreamed of witnessing from the adults around me. I felt a pang of envy.

"And you loved your grandmother very much too?" That was clear to me, but I wanted to hear more.

"She was an extraordinarily compassionate person with a gift for looking after people. People and their plights were important to her. And she had a very clear idea about what she could do or not do for them. She had a very special relationship with her husband, my grandfather. Hugh Edward Cotterill." He paused. "She loved him to bits. They had a very tender relationship despite the fact that Hugh was an alcoholic and, in later in life, a homosexual. I feel very touched by that. There was every reason for her to eject him from her life and say a man who comes home at midnight dead drunk and naked is not someone I want to live with. Instead, she was so wonderfully accepting of who he was, despite all the difficulties."

I found this hard to fathom and wondered whether Godfrey's grandfather was physically abusive. If not, then the strength of his grandmother's love perhaps enabled her to be tolerant.

"Was he violent at all, or aggressive?"

"No, he was the gentlest man on earth. Between the world wars, my grandfather was a major in the British Army and posted to India, where they lived in the officer's quarters in New Delhi. He saw first-hand how the British treated the local population and understood it was not ethical. My grandmother had staff, including a dresser. Because of her rank, she wasn't allowed to dress herself. She hated that. Over the course of their time in India, they both learned to hate the British and love the Indians. She made lots of local friends and contacts before they returned home. When I was very small, during and right after the war, these friends would come and stay with her. Interesting people: philosophers, men of letters, thinkers. It was great to see her with them. And them with her."

Godfrey's story triggered a memory of my own. When I was tiny, my parents rented an upstairs bedsit in an Oxford townhouse owned by a Pakistani family. All twelve of them lived on the ground floor. Vivid images of colourful saris, long, black plaited hair, and sparkling jewellery twinkled in my mind. Keeping my eyes on the road, I also remembered the exact day I first had such a flashback. In 1985, I had walked into an Indian grocery store in Berlin and the aroma of the spices reminded me of the mild curries and chapatis the women downstairs used to feed me whenever they got the chance. That specific memory was the start of a year-long journey to uncover many suppressed images and feelings from my childhood.

"So, your grandmother was very social?"

"She enjoyed interacting with people. When I was in Cambridge, she founded the Teilhard de Chardin Society, which was a very outgoing movement and I was proud of her."

As Godfrey began to explain who Pierre Teilhard de Chardin was – a French Jesuit, theologian and scientist – and his theory of spiritual evolution, we rounded a corner and I pressed my foot on the brakes. The lane was only wide enough for a single car or tractor to pass through at one time and ahead of us a large SUV with a European number plate had stopped. We got out to see what the hold-up was. Ahead, a herd of bleating sheep jostled slowly up the road. We sat back in the car with the doors open. This was going to take a while.

"Where was she from?"

"My grandmother's mother was Irish, married to a Protestant clergyman called Mr English. My grandmother's in-laws were Huguenots and had fled France for England. I have German ancestry too on my mother's side. One of them was called Frederick Huth. He was originally the son of a serf but was sent to Hamburg by a Protestant pastor who thought he was gifted and wanted him to receive an education. Sometime in the eighteenth century, he left Hamburg for London and then Bilbao, where he met his Spanish wife-to-be. Frederick eventually founded the Huth Bank in London in the early nineteenth century, became quite rich actually and was financial advisor to the Spanish queen. His bank was absorbed in the thirties and eventually merged into the Royal Bank of Scotland. I've visited the little town of Harseveld, where he came from, and there is a bronze statue of him in the town centre because he financed the public library, which is still in use today."

Thinking about how we are all a mix of nationalities and how interconnected that makes us, our conversation shifted to how we perceive people as enemies, friends or family, and how we make judgements about them.

"I grew up with this notion that some nationalities were inferior human beings," Godfrey said with a sigh. "My father obviously hated the Germans because, well, we all had to hate the Germans during and after the war, although my mother was part German. He hated the French because, well, they were French. And he hated Americans because he believed they couldn't think.

After the war I can remember my father saying something like, 'The British won the war, despite the bungling Americans!' He claimed that the Americans shot down more British planes near Iceland than the Germans did. He was contemptuous of Americans, maybe more so than of Germans. He said that American airmen were cowboys. In his mind, you had to put powerful aircraft in the hands of public-school educated Englishmen who flew them and became heroes.

When I began working in an American company, I heard an American talking about some linguistic research in a very intelligent way and he, of course, had an American accent and I thought, 'That's funny, he's got an American accent but what he's saying is intelligent and interesting!'"

We burst out laughing at the silliness of our assumptions.

Godfrey added, "And by that time I was twenty-eight!" He shook his head. "That wrong-headed prejudice stayed with me all that time until life proved it was completely divorced from reality."

"And what did your father say about Germans?"

I had become painfully aware of the anti-German sentiment still alive in Britain in the early 1980's when I left England to work in Berlin as an au-pair for a year. I had received farewells accompanied with 'jokes' about Hitler. In 1985, I was still there, living in a shared apartment. I remember I spent that particularly rainy summer glued to my TV watching a German documentary series called 'Forty Years After' produced to commemorate the fortieth anniversary of the end of the Second World War. I immersed myself in this period of German history, reading interviews with witnesses, learning the true stories behind the folk involved, those who were victimised or swayed politically to support the Nazis, or resist them, and I listened to historical coverage. I found myself in awe of the German people's willingness to reflect critically on deep ethical issues, and to understand the psychology behind mass indoctrination, persecution, misuse of power and the intricacies of reconciliation. Growing up in

Britain, I had never experienced this kind of dedication to critical contemplation of British history and political trends.

Back in the car, Godfrey continued: "At that time, during the war, it was the done thing to hate the German people because of the atrocities the Nazis were perpetrating on the continent and the bombing raids on London, Coventry and Liverpool. I never held those stereotypical images of Germans myself, although I feared the bombs falling from the sky.

And then after the war, there were German POWs [prisoners of war] still in camps in England. Both my parents thought that they should be allowed to work, and people like my parents needed the help. On the farm, we employed two Germans for a while after the war ended. One of them was called Walter, and I can still see the fear on his face when he accidentally let the axe slip while he was chopping wood and injured his foot. He wasn't worried so much about his injury, the pain and risk of infection, as the damage he'd done to his British Army-issue boots and the trouble he'd get into."

I smiled in recognition. In the decades since I first arrived in Berlin, I have had to learn not to feel afraid when I interact with German authorities. Simply registering for a residence permit every year used to leave me tearful. I am still uneasy talking to policemen with their pistols perched visibly on their hips. Today, I speak German fluently but remember well when I first arrived, the difficulty I had communicating with staff in state agencies, at the post office or in shops. At that time, customer service was an alien concept and Berliners especially had a reputation for being particularly rude. The peaceful ending of the post-war division of Germany and reconciliation has provided another rich seam for Germans to mine their psyche. There was a strong energy to reunite and also examine the truth and secrets of the past. It wasn't easy. There was friction and bad feeling. But once again, the willingness of German society to self-critically discuss their history, while remaining mostly respectful of others' experiences, has impressed me deeply and indeed formed the person I am today, unafraid to name controversy or contradictions and speak truth to power.

The SUV parked in the road began to inch forward. We pulled our doors closed and I put the car into gear. The presence of Germans in post-war Britain made me think of the Irish community in England that I grew up in. Despite political differences back home, its members were friendly with each other. Just hearing another Irish accent would open my parents' hearts so easily that, to this day, if I catch an Irish lilt in someone's voice, I will turn to smile at them and seek a chat. As a child, I thought everyone who was Irish knew every other Irish person, or someone from their family. Any Irish visitors to our home were met with home-baked soda bread, apple pie, biscuits, cake, and if you stayed long enough, out came the Irish stew, or lamb chops with potato and turnip mash with beans, carrots and sprouts, even if that meant we only had toast for the rest of the week.

The adults who visited our home never spoke about 'The Troubles'. Any talk of religion or politics was kept for the Irish Centres, where I was not allowed to go ("Too many Catholics," my mother replied when I begged to join my friends at Irish dance classes). But news from the homeland was important and anyone returning from a visit was invited around to share updates on 'life back home'. Often people carried messages on behalf of shared acquaintances.

And then, after the Bloody Sunday massacre of January 1972 when British soldiers killed twenty-six civilian protesters and then Bloody Friday, when the IRA (Irish Republican Army) planted at least twenty bombs in Belfast that exploded within two hours, the atmosphere began to change. I began to understand why it was dangerous for my parents to go home. And then, in 1974, when the

IRA blew up two pubs in Birmingham, killing twenty-one people, the ease that existed between the Irish abroad began to stiffen. At the same time, there was a growing sense that Irish people weren't welcome in England. Desperate to fit in with my pals, I never developed an Irish accent.

So, I was curious about the presence of these enemy alien POWs in post-war Britain. What was their life like?

"Where did they live?"

"They didn't stay in the house. They came to work, ate lunch with us or brought their own, and left again later. It strikes me now how open my parents were. It wasn't forced labour; my parents wanted to give them employment. I can remember them working in the fields, woods and on the farm and they didn't look stressed. They spoke with everyone freely, had conversations in German with my mother, who had spent a year at a German boarding school as a young girl. My father never came across to me as a bossy boss. He would hand them tasks and then go off to do his own work. It seemed very, very possible, despite the recent hostility between these two nations, that everyone could work and live together."

The car ahead accelerated and we were on our way again.

"And what about your mother? Was there any reaction in the village to her being able to speak German?"

"I don't remember anything. The sentiment was, the war is over and it's time to make friends again." Godfrey took a breath, apparently considering what he was going to say. "The issue with my mother and father was how they saw themselves as different."

"How do you mean?"

"My father had Irish blood but was brought up in England and felt very English: he had no time or consideration for 'otherness'. Anybody who was different was an enemy, and in his view, there were lots of enemies in England. Anybody who spoke differently from us or didn't meet our standards was an enemy. But then of course, when we didn't meet the standards of our own family, that was painful."

Godfrey recognised the question mark on my face and continued. "My father had been raised until about the age of fifteen in the lap of luxury in Northumberland. The family owned the Spencer Iron & Steel Company that made a fortune in the First World War. Its steel business, John Spencer & Sons, helped build the railway system in Belgium and in the railway museum there you'll find a huge pair of drive wheels dating back to the 1860s with the name engraved on the hubs.

When my father married my mother, a Catholic, he became a family outcast. And when he became Catholic himself, they wanted nothing more to do with him at all."

I nodded, understanding completely the impact of that age-old sectarian antagonism.

"Banished, our family was impoverished upper-class. The Spencer line includes earls and dukes and a direct link, albeit illegitimate, to the House of Stuart. In the seventeenth century, along one branch of the Spencer family, we're connected to the family of Princess Diana."

Hearing the word 'impoverished' made me smile wryly. The underlying privilege behind this choice of vocabulary created a schism in the connection I had been feeling toward Godfrey. Our experiences of poverty, expulsion and 'otherness' were miles apart.

"So, you're related to the future King of England!"

Godfrey and I giggled again.

"Yes, we talk about 'our cousins'!"

For a moment, I felt special to have Godfrey as my travelling companion, then smiled at myself, feeling silly. I had met real nobility before. After having received a scholarship to a private school for girls when I was nine, I was familiar with the upper classes and the contrast between my working-class and farming background and theirs. Some of my friends at school were the daughters of aristocrats, which was a little overwhelming at first, especially as I kept my family history close to my heart. But I had benefitted deeply from my education, and not just academically, but in terms of learning respect, discipline and culture too.

At the next little village, we stopped to take a proper break and stretch our legs. The leaves on the trees were turning red and gold as the season shifted from summer to autumn. As my eyes wandered over the gently sloping hills dotted with sheep and grey, tumbling rocks and stones, it occurred to me in the silence that this land had seen a lot of conflict over the millennia: Roman invaders, Anglo-Norman battles, fighting during the English Civil War and the creation of a short-lived English republic in the seventeenth century. I looked at Godfrey and felt another rush of gratitude at hearing his first-person account of that more recent conflict, the Second World War.

I turned to him, remembering the topic of the NVC retreat we were heading to. "Do you think the end of the war heralded a time of greater compassion?"

"Yep." He paused. "I think that my own sense of compassion was very much nurtured by the relationships I had with the farm animals and our ponies. My younger sister was the same. I remember Mary saying that she had only one confidante in life and that was her Shetland pony. She would put her arms around the pony's neck and she ..." Godfrey's voice cracked and he fumbled in his pocket for his handkerchief. He cleared his throat. "It was so unconditional, that relationship. Mary remembers the softness of the pony's mane, the warmth of its body and how peaceful she became as she told her stories to the pony. My sister told that pony everything. It was a great resource for... for getting everything off her chest."

I sighed, quietly recalling the dog I was given as a gift for Christmas at the age of nine, who would lick the tears off my face as I took refuge in my bedroom from the adult world. Unconditional love was indeed the best solace for heartbreak.

Godfrey too seemed lost in memory. "I had a pony, John-John, and my older sister had one too. John-John was quite a bucker. We would ride him in the field together and would laugh until John-John tossed one of us, or both of us, off. That was great fun, such a lovely memory. The pony wasn't vicious. He was sending us a message: you're on my back, there's no saddle or bridle, so you're not staying on! In actual fact, that was the pony that I rode to primary school."

I looked at him, eyebrows raised.

"We lived about three miles from the school and I used to cycle. I played a game with myself, where I timed the journey on my watch and tried to get there faster each time otherwise, I told myself, I was a hopeless case. This might have been the cause of my heart problem. I developed arrhythmia, an irregular heartbeat, which tired me out. My parents decided to send me to school on horseback. I would ride there and leave the pony in a stable at a local farm just behind the church. The farmer's name was Fairs. Sometimes I would arrive early and take a swim in the North Sea before school. There are two occasions I remember when I didn't actually go to school. On one of those, I was riding the pony past another farm and saw a flock of turkeys in a field. When they saw us coming, they rushed for the courtyard, gobbling, and John-John reared and galloped home. The second time, it was autumn and the fields were cut to stubble. Suddenly, a grey carpet moved across the land. There were hundreds of rabbits – that was the time before myxomatosis – and they were rife. So once again John-John, my pony, upped and headed home.

And I loved my yellow Labrador, Dilly. She had belonged to a policeman who took her shooting, where she was meant to retrieve the birds or rabbits that he shot. She didn't, because she was gun-shy. Every time he fired a shot, she panicked and ran home. The man was going to put her down, so my mother said I could have her. In the night, the dog used to creep upstairs and not just jump onto my bed but get in it and lie against my back and slowly push me out. My mother would find me in the morning, hanging off the edge of the mattress, much to the amusement of everyone. There was no consideration of hygiene. If Godfrey wanted to sleep with his dog, that was fine by my parents. That was very sweet."

We turned into the car park of the country manor, where we were due to start the retreat with an introductory meeting that evening. Although I was excited to begin and meet the other participants, we sat in silence for a while in the stationary car. I felt unwilling to leave the intimacy of the space we had created, aware that as soon as we opened the doors and stepped out, the fresh air would dilute the magic of our shared memories. I hoped there was a new, communal space of intimacy and vulnerability awaiting us in the grand building in front of us. The same, but different.

CHAPTER 4

AN EXCEPTIONAL CHILDHOOD

C limbing back into the car, I felt spent of energy and deeply calm. During the week in Wales, we had deepened our compassionate listening skills. The retreat, organised by a trainer called Gayano, the gentlest soul ever, had been advertised as the inspiring teaching team's last time 'training the trainers'. It drew an array of participants from around twenty different countries all with different levels of NVC training experience. Some were beginners and others like Godfrey and I had decades of teaching experience behind them. I was excited to meet Robert, a trainer from the US, who took a more spiritual approach to NVC, and Gina from the UK, who had developed a process called NVC 'dance floors', in which, using cards placed on the floor, you map out an issue and analyse it by physically moving through it.

I felt free. The earlier training in Montolieu had inspired me to expand my skillset. I was also liberated from the confines of a long-term relationship in which my partner had distrusted my desire to travel and learn. I have always loved being a student in a safe learning environment. As a child, such spaces were a huge resource for me.

As an adult I've relished every chance to replicate this experience. Indeed, during my first decade in Berlin, I obtained four different professional qualifications alongside a masters in psychology. I am a self-described 'learning junkie' who believes you don't know what you don't know until you learn it.

That week in Wales, we examined our strengths and weaknesses as trainers, learning new teaching paradigms, understanding group dynamics, practising presentations and difficult dialogues, sharing challenging teaching moments and also reflecting on our core beliefs and our inner critics, which in the NVC world we call 'jackals'. The atmosphere at the retreat was supportive and full of friendship. Not for the first time, it fascinated me how a large group of people, thirty or so in our case, quickly came to communicate with clarity and trust and could hold any emotion – anger, fear, despair, sadness, shame, joy, confusion, and feelings of mourning and celebration. United in our overall goals of transformation, deep understanding and connection with ourselves and others, students were often to be found sitting on comfy armchairs in front of the open fire, huddled on elegant polished oak staircases or gathered in groups in the gardens, talking, listening and learning, coaching each other in the process of Nonviolent Communication and giving and receiving feedback.

Over the week, I had become friendly with one of the staff who worked at the manor house hosting the training, a young man who came from a village near Oxford, close to where I had grown up. One evening he took me aside and asked what it was we were actually learning here. After I explained briefly the idea behind Nonviolent Communication, that it was about empathy, compassion and conflict resolution, learning to express emotion without blame or criticism, listening and understanding feelings and needs, both within ourselves and in others, he looked quite relieved and said, "Oh, I see, I thought you were all here to learn how to cry better."

I smiled. I hadn't considered how we must look to an 'outsider'.

Pulling out of the driveway, on the start of the journey back to Heathrow, via Reading where I would drop off Godfrey, I told him about that conversation. He laughed heartily and began to tell me about his experience of the retreat and the inner child work he had done. I was keen to hear about it as we hadn't had much time to chat in private during the dynamic training.

"Why do you think you were a loner as a child Godfrey?" I asked.

"The atmosphere in society back then was oppressive. If I look at my mother with all of her attention to duty, truth, to virtue, it was a big constraint." We drove slowly down the narrow country road with the afternoon sun hanging low in the sky while Godfrey led us back into his childhood. "And when I look at my father's 'power-over', domineering tactics, screaming to get what he wanted, then my brother Hugh, who luckily wasn't home very often, bullying me physically, I understand why I went into some sort of a shell. I was safer there. If you keep a low profile you won't get screamed at, hit or lectured."

It sounded very sad to me. I knew that safer shell, having lost my gang when I started at the private school. Around that time, we moved away from the council estate and kept moving for the next four years, finally settling in Northampton. My safe place became the classroom, the library and any extracurricular activity that was available.

"Did you have any friends, Godfrey?"

"They were few and far between. No doubt I grew up to believe that you couldn't trust people. I couldn't trust my father, mother or elder brother. I very much trusted my elder sister, Sabina, though. She was two and a half years older than me. We were very much like twins and had a lot of fun together. She didn't bully me, didn't want to, we were the same physical size, and had the same interests. She loved the horses in the same way I did. We rode a lot together. I remember one day the parish priest came round to visit my mother. As soon as she was distracted by his arrival, we bolted through a window, saddled up our ponies and rode off through the forest. That was an act of rebellion that surely would be paid for later when my father came home and learned about it. He only had to raise his voice and I, at least, felt I was in danger of death. I can't remember how Sabina received his anger. I imagine she was tougher than me; she was older after all."

"Was your mother embarrassed by your behaviour, that you left when the priest visited?"

"I think it was two things for her: she was embarrassed, but also she must have been feeling very proud to have two children who would take the law into their own hands."

"Being independent?"

"Yes, at that time, around 1946-48, we were being home-schooled by our mother and grandmother, who received textbooks and materials from the Parent National Education Union, I think it was called. I didn't go back to actual school until I was eight. And then I was a bit of a loner; I didn't mix. There wasn't anybody to mix with! So, I spent my time falling intensely in love with one girl after another and following the object of my desire around, stuck to them like a limpet mine. One girl was from a neighbouring farm. I would accompany her back home on my bicycle; it wasn't much of a detour. I have no memory of other boys in primary school."

Reflecting on what I'd learned and heard over the past week, I asked, "Your grandmother, Dorothy, was she the only one who showed you compassion as a child?"

"Yes. No, there was a very lovely woman who was both the headmistress and teacher at my primary school, Miss Semence. She taught a school of twenty-six pupils all together; some were in their last year of primary school taking the Eleven-Plus exam to get into grammar school, and others who were in kindergarten! We were all taught in the same room. She was absolutely amazing. Her ability to relate to people was just out of this world. She could keep everybody keen and interested in learning different things. How she did that, I don't know. She lived in a little bungalow up above the cliff with her mother. She was so devoted to her schoolchildren that I think that she had a one hundred percent success rate in exams. Not one of her pupils failed the Eleven-Plus!"

"I remember teachers like that," I said. "Unmarried, tweed suits, sensible brown shoes, absolutely devoted and passionate." That same commitment has inspired me as a teacher. We smiled at each other, nodding silently.

"Then in the autumn term of 1950, I was sent to Catholic boarding school in Walsingham. There, there were only boys."

Travelling with Godfrey was like picking up a familiar book at bedtime and delving back into the story. Our conversation flowed back and forth and before I knew it, the towers of the Severn Bridge appeared ahead once again, looped together with thick suspension cables, a heart-lifting sight. As we crossed, my stomach began to think about food. By then I knew Godfrey well enough to know he had an amazing capacity to go without food for long periods of time without feeling hungry at all, and then, when presented with a plate of something delicious, would wolf it down like there was no tomorrow. I had also noticed that he became more agitated in the car if he hadn't eaten for a couple of hours and had begun to include regular stops in our itinerary.

I turned off the motorway and slowed down as we entered the suburban streets of Stoke Gifford, looking for some 'pub grub'. Settled at a table close to the window in a typical English establishment we had found, we were delighted by its menu of roast beef, Yorkshire pudding, peas and chips. Classic pub food. I was tempted to order a half pint of scrumpy, a very potent cider typical in the west of England, to go with it, but I resisted. I had always upheld a strict 'no drink and drive' policy.

As we waited for our food to arrive, a group of schoolboys wearing blazers and ties passed by on the pavement outside. I smiled. School uniform was such a huge part of my childhood. I was very grateful to wear one as it meant the other children at my private school could not tell that I was there on a scholarship and that my family's financial circumstances were vastly different from theirs. My uniform was very distinctive: a navy-blue blazer with the school emblem on the pocket, a blouse and blue jumper and an A-lined checked skirt that had to fall below the knee. It was expensive and, washed and diligently ironed every weekend, had to last the entire school year. Every summer holiday we would wait impatiently for the check from the scholarship fund to finally arrive, after all my friends already had bought their new uniforms. Only my cheap shoes and satchel signalled our reduced circumstances.

However, imagining the bus ride home to the council estate, it became apparent that I would stand out and be at risk of bullying or worse, and that prompted our move to a village outside Oxford, with the school's assistance.

I was to learn from my conversations with Godfrey that attending school surrounded by wealthy pupils and lacking funds ourselves was an experience we shared. I took the bus to school or rode my bicycle, while most of the other girls were dropped off by car, some chauffeur driven after a weekend in Paris or spending the school holidays in the south of France. In contrast, I spent my Saturday mornings completing my newspaper delivery round and Sunday mornings cleaning a kindergarten (officially contracted to my mother). From the age of thirteen, I worked as a dishwasher at weekends and then later, I had an after-school job in the office of a toyshop, before working three nights a week as a waitress from the age of sixteen. I straddled two seemingly incompatible class structures. It put me in good stead in later life by enabling me to resonate with those living a 'life of luxury', while simultaneously remembering the austerity of my early years.

"What was your uniform like Godfrey?" I asked.

"I was supposed to wear grey flannels. My mother would not buy that material because it was so fragile. She found a grey-and-black herringbone tweed wool instead, which if you looked at it with your eyes half-closed, could be grey flannel. When I arrived wearing my uniform, the headmaster said, 'You can't wear that!' Then, I think, he realised we didn't have the money. My uniform was never talked about again. It was touching and painful at the same time. I was about eleven years old then."

This story softened the disconnection I had previously felt on our journey down when he spoke of being the impoverished upper-class. The feeling of shame and secrecy about being poor is something that penetrates every cell of your body and I am convinced can only be fully understood if you have experienced it personally. When someone recognises you and spares you embarrassment, the warmth of gratitude and relief is palpable. I nodded in agreement, while he continued.

"But I wasn't there long. The following February the Walsingham parish priest contacted my parents and told them to remove me from the school. The headmaster, it turned out, was homosexual – although that wasn't widely known at the time – and had hired other male teachers who were interested in little boys and watched them take their baths. I had no idea anything was going on. No one ever approached or even looked at me. I left to attend day school, and then two years later, I was sent to another Catholic boarding school, St Joseph's College, in Ipswich. Again, I was a loner. I can remember crying myself to sleep because my dog wasn't with me on the bed."

Godfrey dabbed tears away from his eyes with a handkerchief.

"Did you have any friends there?"

"There was one boy who was a very talented artist, Tom. We became accomplices. Once, we must have been sixteen, we were playing inside with very powerful water pistols. One of the monks, a young cocky brother, discovered us and confiscated them. Through the window of his room, we spotted our pistols and went in to retrieve them. It was a huge intrusion into his privacy. He reported us to the headmaster, who called us into his office.

The headmaster was a top-class human being, a real 'mensch'. That's one German word I love. It describes someone's humanity. He had a keen eye for distress. He always wanted people to grow, to become more autonomous.

He told us that the brother wanted to beat us. He had tried to dissuade him by suggesting the alternative punishment of banning us from tennis for some time, but the young monk had insisted he had the right. And he gave us 'six of the best', beating us with a stick stripped of its bark so it would hurt more. It was a horrific experience that we understand now as a form of abuse. The pain was the worst. In the classroom after, I could barely sit down. The bruises were still there two weeks later. I thought about telling my parents, but didn't because I thought they would side with the teacher. I thought of telling the police, but I reasoned that all the grown-ups were allies and in cahoots with each other. After the beating, the monk tried to be nice to us, shake our hands. Tom and I just ignored him, walked away, before we caved in about a month after, accepting his handshake.

Later, the headmaster promoted me to head of house. He told me, 'I hope this will keep you out of mischief!' I thought that was so big-hearted and clever of him, because now that I had responsibilities, what else could I do but behave?!"

I felt a warm rush of recognition. Many of my teachers have served as excellent role models for my entire life. They introduced me to literature, history, classical music, languages, art history and drama, and I was a keen student. I'm still in touch with one of them, my German teacher Marilyn, who played a huge role in supporting me through my difficult teenage years.

"It sounds like there was some real comradery there between you and Tom?"

"I had good times with Tom. We also started a tennis club. We plotted the court and marked it out and the school supplied the net. It was great fun. We were the only ones in the school to have motorbikes. I sold him my granny's Corgi and I had my brother's Sunbeam, which was very powerful. We were allowed to keep the bikes in a brick shed. One day, Tom and I were in there and had locked the door to stop any intruders. One of the other pupils, a big chap, tried to get in. He put his shoulder to the door and broke it down. I was so enraged I rushed at him and I hit him in the stomach with my head, grabbed him and threw him into a bed of nettles. I never knew I could do a thing like that, something so violent. I was like a tower of muscle and sinew. I was so angry! You can't break down the door to my shed, that's my shed!"

I was enthralled by an image of a young Godfrey charging like a bull at someone, out of control, and my mouth dropped open in disbelief. It was so out of character, so different to how he portrayed himself. I began to laugh.

"I also had a good time playing rugby," Godfrey's face relaxed. "I used to be able to drop-kick a goal from behind the half-way line. I played at fly-half. I was very fast over short distances and it was likely if I got the ball that there would be a try at the end of my run."

We had almost finished our lunches. I looked at my companion sitting opposite me as he began to cry again. I gave him my full presence, sitting there in silence with him, opening my heart and emptying my mind of any chatter or commentary. I was simply being in the moment, witnessing his vulnerability, embracing his experience without encroaching on his space, remembering to withhold any advice, to ignore any distraction, to hold back any comforting sounds or corrections, simply trusting the moment and knowing words would come if necessary. And they did. Godfrey snorted loudly into his handkerchief, looked up at me, shrugged his shoulders, his eyes searching mine, and let out a big sigh.

He whispered, "Thank you."

We held each other's gaze for a while, smiling gently in recognition.

"What moves you recounting that story?" I asked quietly.

"Because it's positive and there's wasn't so much of that in my childhood." Godfrey dried his face on a handkerchief. "But there were good times. I got selected by the Eastern Counties, which is Essex, Suffolk and Norfolk, to play in the under-eighteens' rugby team as fly-half. I remember playing one of the worst games of my life." He chuckled. "It was drizzling and the earth on the pitch was very slippery. I couldn't catch or pass the ball; it was an absolute tragedy. After that I played for the local men's team, Lowestoft and Yarmouth. The bit I hated most was the bit they loved the most, which was drinking in the pub after the match. I just used to go home; I didn't want to be there, because drink meant drunk and that was my father and that was dangerous. I didn't want to be like that."

"We both have witnessed so much violence in our childhoods. How have you grown up not to be a violent person?"

Godfrey stared out the window for a moment. "I think the violence in me is well hidden. When I became head of department of the interpreters' school at the university, I asked to have a couple of hours at the beginning of each year to spend warning the new students what the job of interpreting entailed to help them make a decision about whether they would want to stay and do those studies. I had one hundred and forty people for two hours a week. At one lecture, I noticed three people at the back having a conversation. I stopped speaking and just looked at them. One hundred and thirty-seven people looked at them with me as they continued to chat until one nudged the other and they stopped. It wasn't until about five years later that I understood how scary I was as a teacher. When something makes me angry, I can disappear inside and look out at the world with steel in my eyes."

As Godfrey spoke, it occurred to me that in lots of his stories, he was the odd one out or the exception to the rule. The only one to bear his father's anger; the only one in his family allowed a dog; the only pupil to ride to school on a pony or wear a different school uniform. I put this to him.

He grinned. "The other exception was that I was the only boy at school who didn't have a cap."

"Why was that?"

"Because they didn't make caps that big!"

"Are you serious?" I giggled.

"Yes, I was nicknamed Big Head."

We burst out laughing.

"It was just a nickname. I didn't take offence. My father called me Professor Earwig and my brother adopted that too. If ever I said something philosophical, one of them would say, 'Oh yes, Professor Earwig has his theories of course'. It was quite amusing because I did have my theories that left them stumped, and me too sometimes!" He smiled. "But I realised later that I used this trick of being very analytical to keep people at bay, to stop them getting to know me, and to prevent me from getting to know me. I stayed focused on the outside because the inside was too painful."

Godfrey coughed quietly. I sipped my tea. "So, you were lonely as a child?"

"I never felt lonely because I was always so busy – with frogs in the water, or with the dog, the pony, lots of survival tactics. Things could have been worse. When I was a child, we'd just been through the war, which was as bad as life could get, so anything else had to be better than that. Better than a poke in the eye with a burnt stick, as they say!"

Then and now, I have never heard anyone but Godfrey use this expression.

We left the warmth of the pub and headed down the street. It started to pour with rain. "It never rains if I have the umbrella on me!" Godfrey said as we ran toward the car.

As the drops hit my face, I thought about the Welsh rain showers that had interspersed our week, somehow mirroring the ample flow of tears shed in the manor house. I gripped Godfrey's arm tighter as we hurried on.

CHAPTER 5

ON THE MOVE

I next saw Godfrey about six months after our retreat in Wales. In between, we had been keeping in touch with Skype calls. Again, we met in England, where he had moved after a swift and emotionally dishevelling divorce from his third wife. He wanted to be closer to his eldest daughter Virginia and her gentle, fun-loving husband Matthew. They lived in a seventeenth-century cottage they had refurbished in the Chilterns, close to where I had spent my earliest childhood years. They had been so happy to introduce Godfrey to their circle of friends and to integrate him into their daily lives, but he had missed Belgium.

After living abroad for more than fifty years, he was still working all over Europe, India and the United States and rarely spent time at his English house. He jokingly told me that if he calculated the number of hours he had actually spent at home and compared it to the rent, it cost him around £500 an hour to stay there.

So, he had decided to move back to Belgium. And I offered to help him pack up his belongings. Our friendship had deepened into a mini mutual support group. We were both recovering from the breakup of long-term relationships and starting out on new ventures. It was so easy to share our stories, worries or sorrows, and to bounce ideas off each other for professional developments. Our individual life skills complemented each other. Godfrey's ease with entering into the unknown fascinated me, gave me courage. My ability to structure, plan, and divide tasks into bite-size chunks combined with precision and reliability was somewhat beyond him. So, when I heard his sighs and overwhelm regarding his pending move, I gladly offered to help. I had the time and could also see some old friends in the UK.

As I walked into the Arrivals Hall at Luton Airport, an hour north of London, I caught sight of Godfrey and we exchanged a brief hug and peck on the cheek.

We hurried to his car as it began to rain. This time Godfrey was the driver. I was relieved. He had brought his car over from Belgium and the driver's seat was on the left-hand side. Used to driving in Germany, I was uncertain if I would be able to remember to keep on the correct side of the road if I drove with the gear stick in my right hand. And I was glad to have a rest, although I did wonder whether Godfrey would be able to drive the entire one-and-half-hour's journey back to his house. I rested back in the passenger seat and decided I would keep him chatting.

As I watched the countryside pass by, I mentioned that it was a shame I hadn't caught a flight from Berlin to Stanstead Airport instead. "We could have visited Cambridge for the day, had a walk around the colleges and had tea."

I was curious about his university days there.

Godfrey glanced at me, horrified. "But that would have been absolutely out of the way and taken us ages!"

No more time at the wheel than necessary was his preference. "Do you ever go back there to visit?"

"Not since I moved to Belgium. And that was fifty years ago."

"What was it like living with your grandmother there when you were an undergraduate?"

"We had a very loving relationship because she didn't weigh on me in any way. Obviously, I did things for her, shopping, household chores and so on. I wanted to. She was very good to me, providing space and conversation. It was a very privileged place to be and she helped me study. I never had a lonely moment. I think she prepared all of the meals. She didn't place any responsibilities on me. I had a grant and everything was paid for, I had about £150 a term, but I didn't need anything."

I leaned back in the seat and closed my eyes, enjoying being driven and imagining Godfrey and other young students scurrying around ancient quads looking like characters from an early Agatha Christie novel, all of which I had read with delight. I smiled to myself, realising the setting for his student days would have been the sixties, but an image of him with long hair, in paisley shirts, denims and love beads jarred in my head. I was sure young Oxbridge students were still wearing old-fashioned tweed jackets then, even if their trousers were more like to have been drain-pipes. I thought of asking him when he suddenly swerved away from an overtaking lorry and swore loudly when he saw the Spanish number plate.

"Qué cabrón!"

I knew Godfrey had spent six months in Madrid before he went up to university and could speak Spanish so well that people asked him which part of the country he was from.

"You studied Spanish at Cambridge?" I asked, trying to calm him down and take his mind off the heavy traffic

"Yes, and English." He took a deep breath. "I was taught Spanish by a Professor Wilson, who had written something like thirty-six volumes on Spanish literature and was sought after as a world expert. His spoken Spanish though was quite hilarious. He spoke with such a strong English accent that you'd recognise it even if you didn't speak the language. He was totally unable to express himself phonetically, although he could write Spanish like a Spaniard."

I knew by then that Godfrey loved to pick up on language anomalies. I was to learn later he was also a stickler for perfection when proof-reading.

Then Godfrey's face dropped. "About a decade after Cambridge, I was visiting my sister in Irun where she lived with her Spanish husband, when my eight-year-old niece informed me, 'Tu hablas muy mal!' – You speak Spanish really badly. That sort of set the record straight about my being invisibly bilingual."

I snorted with laughter. I loved Godfrey's dry sense of humour and ability to make fun of himself.

Godfrey shook his head at the memory.

I told him about my French teacher at school, Mr Oliver, a very animated and fun-loving young man with wiry red hair and beard, who wore colourful checked suits and a bow tie. He used to hop around the classroom grunting like a baboon making "ou" "en" and "o" sounds, exasperated at our pronunciation, which left us girls in stitches. I often think of him when I hear French spoken with an English accent.

"I think it's quite common for native English speakers to not be able to lose their accents. You're one of the exceptions there Godfrey. I mean your French is impeccable."

Godfrey stuck his nose in the air in affected pride.

I continued: "Most Brits are instantly identifiable when they speak German. My German teacher Marilyn was an exception. She was such an excellent teacher. She really pounded the rules into us. I still have the grammar diary she made us write. And I do love that once you've learned German grammar, you can improve fast, because there are few exceptions to those rules. So different from French or Spanish."

Godfrey nodded. "Is she why you went to Germany in the first place?"

"Yes. Marilyn was a godsend during my last years at school. She probably saved my life actually with her personal support. Her love of the German language was infectious."

We chatted about our love of languages, teaching methods, sharing anecdotes about listening secretly to conversations in public places and practising different dialects.

Approaching Watford Junction on the M25 motorway, we hit a traffic snarl and ground to a halt. Roadworks.

Godfrey continued on the theme of language: "Once, years later, when I was working for the UN on an agricultural project in Africa, I was asked if I would interpret for a Chilean man into English. It was most embarrassing. There I was with this degree and I just couldn't do it. I was shocked at what I had learned and also forgotten. But then American Spanish is not Castilian Spanish." He raised an eyebrow.

"How did you come to live in Belgium if Spanish was your focus?"

"I took A-level Spanish and French at school for my final exams and fell in love with my French teacher. She, of course, never knew, because you didn't disclose things like that."

"This seems to be a habit of yours, secretly attaching yourself to desirable women." I recalled his story of his primary school days falling in love with one girl after another. "Perhaps falling in love with a native speaker is the most effective way to learn a language," I teased him.

He ignored my comment and continued. "This teacher suggested I attend a workshop in Belgium, hosted by a Dominican monk called Dominique Pire, who had been awarded the Nobel Peace Prize. She thought it would interest me. And I thought, yes, YOU are of interest to me!" Godfrey chuckled. "So, I enrolled. At the last minute, she didn't go, but I did and it was there that I met Rolande, my future wife and the mother of my children."

"Rolande was your first serious romantic relationship?" I was alert and paying full attention now.

"Yes. When I started at university, I used to spend six weeks in Cambridge and then a month in Brussels with Rolande. I spent all my significant holidays in Belgium. When I met Father Pire, the monk, he asked me to work with him as an interpreter, English to French and vice-versa, the following year. I did this for two seasons working alone and almost had a nervous breakdown. I decided there was one thing I would never do in my life, and that was be an interpreter!"

We laughed out loud at the irony of this statement.

"That's a lot to balance, working as an interpreter, studying and your new relationship with Rolande."

"As I finished my studies at Cambridge, two things kept me going. Societies – I was a member of the college debating society and the university Spanish society, as well as a social club where I established some very enriching relationships – and music. I played classical guitar. The workload was tough as I was never a great reader. I enjoyed writing the essays though and the time spent with my supervisors going over the written work. You couldn't invent anything or wriggle through, you had to know your stuff. And I was less involved with my family, so the violence, the anger and bullying disappeared."

"And Rolande?"

"We spent two years courting and married in 1962 in Brussels, just before my last year at Cambridge. I had met her, moved from home to Cambridge, spent one year in college accommodation, then two years as a student living with my grandmother, and then I moved to Brussels in 1963, where I started working for Max Factor in a job set up for me by my new father-in-law."

"How did you feel being married?"

He took a breath. "It was very scary being in a relationship after all I'd experienced. One of my biggest fears as a young boy was sexuality. I still remember my mother saying to me, 'If you lose your virginity while you're at Cambridge, you'll have to deal with me.' I was very affected by that weight of sinfulness."

"Do you mean you felt obliged to get married then?" I was interested. Having grown up surrounded by patchwork families, unmarried couples and single parents, I could not imagine marrying out of duty. Although I had been brought up surrounded by fairy tale images of finding your prince, getting married, having children and living happily ever after, they were in stark contrast to the reality I witnessed around me. I recognised that my schoolfriends' parents' marriages appeared to be happy and steady and wondered if that went hand in hand with financial stability.

My mother's biggest worry was that I would be a teenage mum. She carried the shame of her own experience. And the notion that every woman needed a man to support her financially. Listening to Godfrey, it occurred to me that obligations, conventions, traditions and rules about marriage really have changed over the last forty years. I felt grateful that today, there's more of a focus on forming healthy connections rather than on following social rules.

"I was a follower. It was as if it was Rolande's marriage and I had a walk-on part," Godfrey stated. "My wife had more life experience, she was working, I was still studying at the national library in Brussels for my degree." He took a breath. "It was the kind of library where you never see books on shelves. You ask an employee for what you want, they search for it in the stacks on a separate floor and bring it to you. And you return it before you leave the building, so there are no thefts."

I looked at Godfrey agape. He'd blatantly switched the topic of conversation.

"You'd rather talk about books than romance?"

"OK, I felt very romantic towards Rolande, and was a very tender husband. I was very attentive to what was important to my wife, but had no idea of what was important in a relationship. I was loyal, but more out of a sense of sin, fear of sin. I didn't realise that loyalty was something you could cultivate. When I was being loyal, it was in order to be good.

I had read a book by Gustav Thibault. He wrote that every woman in a romantic relationship with a man is looking for stability and is focused on rearing children. I understood that it was very mean of a man to bring about romantic feelings in a woman without being willing to offer her what she was dreaming of."

"You mean to sleep with her without offering security and children?" I asked.

"Yes. That was a principle propounded in those days. I loved my wife, I wanted to contribute to her happiness, I was a pleaser in that way, a giver and that gave me value, self-worth."

I felt a sentient twang in my chest. Godfrey's description chimed with those fairy tales I had been fed, the romantic idea of being cared for financially, emotionally, by someone who only wishes to please. I sighed inwardly. This Hollywood dream had still left its mark on me despite my independence, the equality I have found in my relationships at all levels, my ability to provide for myself financially, and my awareness that such relationships aren't real.

"It's sounds unbalanced. Where was her empathy for you?" I wondered aloud.

"My wife's mother was probably the most empathic towards me. She ran a funeral parlour, which had a reputation for being the nicest one around. Her success was founded on her ability to listen to people in mourning. She was also very popular amongst the Jewish community, who had elaborate wishes. If she hadn't been so caring, or as Father Pire referred to her, 'une maman mangeuse', a devouring mother, she probably could have lived off that business very well. But as soon as Rolande needed to go somewhere, her mother would drive her there, neglecting her business and making her daughter very dependent on her."

"How was that for you?"

We were close to the turnoff for the M4 motorway heading toward Reading. Godfrey seemed to be a little tired but I didn't wish to halt the flow of our conversation by suggesting we find a place to stop and switch seats. I also sensed a very subtle air of possessiveness about the car.

"As I adapted to life in Belgium, I was very lonely because I was in cosmetics and that IS very cosmetic! I was the administrative assistant to the managing director, looking after the sales team, keeping an eye on price control. I introduced data processing and did all the interfacing between the company and IBM."

"What did your grandmother think of your choices?"

"I think she was happy for me. She was in her seventies then, as I am now. She was an old lady with a walking stick. After I moved to Belgium, she stayed in Cambridge. I came back later when she was killed by a policeman."

"What? Jeez." I tried to catch my breath. "Are you serious?"

"As you know, she was a very religious person." Godfrey's voice was calm, almost quiet. "She was walking across a pedestrian crossing in the dark, in the rain, going to evening mass. This policeman didn't even see her as he drove in his car with his children in the back."

I was speechless. I felt I knew this woman, had been very impressed with her character and how she showed her love for Godfrey. My sadness surprised me. Over the years, I've come to learn that Godfrey has a habit of blurting out tragic information that frequently makes me catch my breath.

Godfrey continued with so much tenderness. "My parents didn't launch any legal proceedings. They didn't want to compromise the policeman's career. What good would it have done my grandmother? By then she was over eighty and it was an easy death; she died on the spot. I loved my parents for that. I didn't see her corpse though, and for a long time it was as if she was away on holiday, or simply unable to meet, just wasn't there, and not as if she'd died."

We drove in silence for a while, meditating on the fragility of life and the importance of saying goodbye. The countryside rolled by outside lit by rays of pale afternoon sunlight. Although Godfrey seemed confident in the driver's seat, his story of the incident in Belgium, him blacking out a few years ago, was very present in my mind. I remained alert.

I caught sight of a sign for Wallingford, a small town in south Oxfordshire my parents and I would visit on Sunday afternoons when I was little. Those were uncharacteristically peaceful outings. The town is also the location for the famed fictional TV series 'Midsomer Murders', which, after I moved to Berlin, I loved watching when I felt sentimental for home.

"I haven't been there since I was a child, can we go?" I asked Godfrey.

"Good idea, let's do that." Godfrey nodded. "It's just a minor detour."

His agreement was a sign he needed a loo break. I knew Godfrey quite well by now.

Strolling over Wallingford Bridge, an impressive medieval structure that crosses the River Thames upstream, we headed for Wallingford Castle Meadows where we looked at the ruins of the former fort, which was demolished in 1652 by Oliver Cromwell. One of the most famous visitors to Wallingford was the highwayman Dick Turpin, a kind of eighteenth-century Robin Hood. Godfrey and I walked arm in arm as he recited The Ballad of Dick Turpin by Alfred Noyes. I was amazed at his ability to recall facts and dates, and how that contrasted with his inability to remember where he had just left his keys.

When we arrived at Godfrey's house, he unpacked some treats we'd bought in Wallingford for supper, ciabatta, cheese and homemade cake, and I toured the place turning on the heating. Moving through the rooms upstairs, dodging boxes and suitcases, I realised there was only one double bed. When Godfrey called up the stairs for me to turn on the radiator in 'the bedroom', did he mean 'the' bedroom where he thought we would both spend the night? I felt a flash of panic, but I remained calm as I descended the staircase.

If Godfrey wished for more intimacy from our relationship, I had not seen that coming. Being able to set clear and safe boundaries was an important part of my private and professional lives, but I too could miss subtle messages. I decided to take more care about not sending ambiguous signs, while also aware that I might be misinterpreting him. I did not wish to dwell on it. Godfrey had been my teacher and was now a good friend to me, and I to him. We were confidantes in a period of personal stress, had shared our childhood stories, which had been traumatic in different ways, and we shared a love of language, nature, NVC and animals. I didn't want to lose that.

In the living room, stepping around more boxes, gadgets and piles of books, I noticed, under the window to the garden, two big soft brown sofa-like chairs that, if pushed together, would simulate a small guest couch. I set my small suitcase next to one, rearranged them, placing a cushion from a dining chair as a pillow. As Godfrey walked in carrying our food on a tray, I said casually, "I'll be fine down here. That's going to be really cosy and warm enough for me."

He looked over to my makeshift sleeping space and nodded silently. The matter was never spoken of again.

As we chatted over supper about plans for the next six days, I began making a schedule in an Excel spreadsheet on my laptop.

The first morning, we visited Godfrey's eldest daughter Virginia and her family. After my own childhood experiences and years of professional welfare work in dysfunctional family constellations, it is always a joy for me to witness a happy, relaxed and caring atmosphere between parents and children. I loved the connection between Godfrey and his daughter and her family. Godfrey speaks French to Virginia, who has been totally deaf from the age of three from meningitis, and she lipreads. It somehow soothes my soul to experience how life can be when the underlying tone of relationships is ease, peace and gentleness. In my memory, Virginia and Matthew's house was full of animals, but there were probably just three dogs, including their shiny black Labrador, Bo, as well as a new puppy, and some cats. Bo made an instant connection with me, or I with her.

After sifting through a pile of footwear by the backdoor to find some Wellingtons that would fit me, we accompanied Matthew and the dogs on a walk through the meadows. While eating a delicious lunch made by Matthew, who did all the cooking, we discussed giving Bo some respite from the new puppy and I was delighted that she was allowed to come and stay with us at Godfrey's house for a couple of days.

Our days were spent in a kind of twilight zone surrounded by boxes and possessions, me wrapping crockery in newspaper, ornaments in bubble wrap, while Godfrey sorted out books to keep and others to give away, interspersed with dog-walking and swapping stories, working really hard to meet Godfrey's removal date. Having taken a week off work, I was glad not to have to constantly answer my phone or check my emails.

Godfrey's grandson, home from university for the Easter break, came to help dispose of some heavier items, but most of the packing, labelling and listing items in each box on a spreadsheet, was left to me. I took charge, while Godfrey, who had set himself the goal of minimising his belongings, spent his time looking through papers, books, agonising over what to keep, and reminiscing. I realised that he was overwhelmed and the energy between us shifted. I became a little bossy with him, guiding him gently but firmly back to a task in hand, noticing his tendency to wander off or wallow in stories, rather than make decisions.

As he dithered over which books to get rid of and which to keep, I suggested a little ritual. I would hand him any three volumes and he could choose only one he wanted to keep. He sighed, he moaned, he deliberated, but I could see he was enjoying the process, having delegated the responsibility for future feelings of loss to me. It felt strange for me to be in charge of the fate of his possessions, but we had a lot of laughs and he thanked me every evening. The scene reminded me of a story he'd told me on one of our trips about a girl he'd met on his first day in kindergarten.

"There was a little girl who saw me busy making circles with a crayon in my left hand. Gently, but firmly, she took the crayon from the left hand and put it in my right hand, and from that minute onwards, I wrote with my right hand. I never called that into question. I must have known that she knew something that I didn't know. And I still do all sorts of things with my left hand, like play tennis and shoot off my left shoulder, for example."

Every afternoon we took Bo for a long country walk, enjoying the fresh air, beautiful parks, squishy footpaths that followed the Thames, steering the dog away from the swans and ducks on the river, navigating narrow lanes with pretty cottages planted on the hillsides. In the little village of Cholsey, we placed some flowers on Agatha Christie's grave. That evening, we entertained ourselves imagining the plot for a murder mystery set at an NVC retreat.

On day six, my friend Claire, a furniture designer, arrived to whisk me off to London. I do love the ease with which British folk can chat politely with strangers. Claire gave Godfrey tips on how best to safely pack up some of his antique furniture. That was all that was left to do.

Tired but impressed by our work, Godfrey and I parted with a hearty hug.

CHAPTER 6

WORK, REST AND PLAY

My sabbatical year had not gone as planned. Instead of spending 2014 travelling, learning and having fun, I spent six months stuck in my flat in Berlin, rarely able to make it down the four flights of stairs to the world outside. I couldn't move my arms or legs without experiencing tremendous pain and was taking lots of medication. I had suffered for years with fibromyalgia, but this time, the diagnosis from my doctors was unclear. My contact with people was reduced to phone and Skype calls, which is how I stayed in touch with Godfrey.

We had decided to write up the stories he'd told me on our journeys and possibly create his biography. The idea gave me some purpose and I could still type with ease. I so looked forward to our weekly calls, filled with gossip, empathy and laughter at each other's daily 'failings', although his move back to Belgium and a new home in Brussels had been a success. He had picked up where he left off six months before, except now he was a divorcee with an abundance of friends and a busy social life, still travelling, facilitating and teaching.

By the summer, I was on the road to recovery. I could drive again if I remembered to take regular rest breaks. Joyful to finally be able to do something exciting during my year off, I decided to take a road trip tracing the coast of Western Europe, letting myself follow every whim on the way, except for one fixed destination - the annual NVC event, the European Intensive Course, in the south of France, my third time.

At the beginning of July, with four weeks to reach Montolieu, I climbed into my little Citroen, and, with the boot packed with camping gear, just in case, an inflatable kayak, snorkel, flippers, books and medicine, off I set. It felt so liberating to be behind the wheel again. I was a confident but cautious driver and loved the challenge of finding the best times and traffic-free routes. I was not in a rush. I had weeks to make it to Brussels, where I would collect Godfrey, who was to be one of the lead trainers once again at the Peace Factory in Montolieu and my passenger on the way.

Before I reached Brussels, an old school-time friend I still kept in touch with, Bert, had decided to take the Eurostar to Amsterdam for a much-needed minibreak. He was my first invited hitchhiker.

Bert and I spent a couple of days catching up on news from home, sightseeing the canals, bridges and markets in Holland's beautiful capital before driving on to Belgium, where I dropped him at the Brussels-Midi/Zuid Train Station and met Godfrey to collect some of his luggage.

Early the next day, I picked Godfrey up at his new home. So that I didn't sit behind the wheel for too long in one stretch, I had scheduled an overnight stop halfway in Le Mans at the home of my lovely Scottish friend Aileen. I had worked for her as an au pair in my early days in Berlin and had felt totally embraced by my new surrogate family. Since then, I had been welcomed into Aileen's home many times and knew she was happy to extend her generosity to Godfrey too, who, like her was a conference interpreter, and like Aileen's gentle giant of a husband, was a former rugby player.

Godfrey and I set off on our six-hour drive in good spirits, although a few hours behind schedule, having spent the previous afternoon repacking the boot and backseat, and then running errands and picking up luggage. This was usually the way. This time, Godfrey had asked if we could also transport the camping gear of another participant who was travelling to the retreat by train. Now I understood why he had so much stuff. As he balanced her camping stove, fuel containers and hand-cranked blender on top of each other in the footwell on the passenger side, I silently wondered who this woman was.

We headed south avoiding the Ring Ouest and taking smaller, quieter roads. Our conversation resumed as if it had never stopped.

"After you got married and moved to Belgium, what was life like? How did you get from Max Factor to NVC?"

"Well, I moved first to IBM. Remember, I'd done the data processing interfacing between the two companies. At IBM, I was part of a team of six and we taught a thing called 'effective international communication'. We would take groups of ten to twelve people, mostly from France, some from Belgium, to England and teach them how to make presentations, chair a meeting, how to listen, that sort of thing. This was from 1968-1979."

"I never cease to be amazed by your memory."

"Now, here's an interesting thing about memory." Godfrey was quickly back in his element, telling stories. "At IBM, we had thirty thousand pupils learning English. We collected statistics galore on them and there was no difference in attainment between a twenty-five-year-old and a fifty-year-old person. Learning ability and memory do not seem to decline with age. I notice this in myself. When I was teaching effective communication in IBM, we would instruct groups of about sixteen people. I was in my thirties then and had quite a lot of difficulty learning the names of the participants."

"I've never noticed that at NVC trainings, quite the opposite in fact."

"Yes, now I work with large groups for only two days and find that after hearing someone's name just once, I remember it. I think it is the difference in the listening. At IBM, I had to learn names, so that was 'have-to' energy. Now when people introduce themselves, they say their name, how they're feeling, and what they would like to take away from the training. I listen to them with huge interest. I am choosing to engage in this work relationship. It's very different. Each person has his or her own special importance."

"Mmm. So, why did you call me Sabine yesterday?" I kept a straight face. Sabine is a very common name in Germany and Godfrey's elder sister happens to be called Sabina.

Godfrey turned to me, horrified.

"I'm just teasing you!"

Passing through Waterloo, the scene of the great nineteenth-century battle between Napoleon's armies and a coalition of forces led by the Duke of Wellington, which put an end to the French emperor's ambitions, Godfrey pointed to the Butte du Lion (Lion's Mound). The monument, completed in 1826 to commemorate the battle, is a huge man-made hill forty-three metres high and capped with a statue of a lion on a plinth, Godfrey explained.

We were back talking about war.

"How did you come to work for NATO [North Atlantic Treaty Organisation]?"

"I was at IBM for ten years and left because they wanted me to move to England. I had two daughters by then and Virginia was doing well at school. Because of her deafness, I didn't want her to have to endure the change and learn English. I'd already stopped talking to her in English myself." Godfrey chuckled. "It's funny that, as an adult, she fell in love with Matthew, an Englishman, and has brought up four children in England, in English, with no help from me at all!"

I smiled remembering the affection between Godfrey, Virginia and Matthew.

Godfrey continued: "But the year before I left IBM, I took a year's sabbatical and went to work at NATO as an interpreter."

"How was that?"

"It was difficult to adjust to being an interpreter rather than teaching communication. In my interview for the role, I said that two people speaking different languages would not be able to communicate at all without an interpreter and enabling them to do so was a thrill. That was the way I lived my eighteen-year career with the organisation – by helping people to communicate. In that particular way, it wasn't very different from my job with IBM."

"But it's quite a switch. How did you hear of the job?"

"I was already working freelance as an interpreter and met an American woman who told me NATO was looking for native English-speakers, so I applied."

"What was it like?" I was curious about Godfrey's experience working for a military organisation. It seemed at odds with his dedication to non-violence. To me, NATO was about the Cold War and hating Russia. Maybe I had misunderstood what the Alliance was about and what working there must be like.

"Did you have to go into the office every morning?" I asked.

"Not every day. The meetings were very technical. For security reasons, I was only given maximum eighteen hours to prepare. That was hard. Working hours were difficult to predict. Sometimes meetings were scheduled to last for days. At other times, I was on call. Sometimes I'd be home in the early afternoon, sometimes quite late. Around then, the NATO allies were very concerned about Soviet expansion plans, possibly into Ukraine or Poland. Every time there were troop movements, members would meet to discuss the organisation's response. And of course, they needed their interpreters."

Godfrey spoke with such ease and lightness, but I was surprised at the level of his involvement in important political discussions. The stakes were high.

As we passed a road sign for Vallée de Sensés, feigning ignorance, I wondered aloud if that could be translated as the 'valley of the senses'. Godfrey was not impressed with my attempt at a joke. In fact, he informed me, it is named after the river La Sensée that crosses the département of Pas-de-Calais. Then he guffawed, recalling a time when an American consultant challenged his translation skills. "He didn't like my English! And I was convinced my translation was the best."

At that time, Godfrey explained, he was working on a NATO relocation project from Paris to near Brussels and wrote the daily minutes of the site construction team.

"So, I produced a document listing the French phrase, my translation and the American's translation and an independent expert who upheld my choices every time!" With a wry smile, he quoted another of his childhood nicknames: "Don't challenge Gobby!"

As we passed by a sign for Amiens, the site of yet more battles in both world wars, I turned to Godfrey.

"Your life has been permeated with war and enemy images. It's so uncanny that you now teach NVC, helping people transform their view of others and enabling them instead to find the common ground of their humanity."

"Yes," he agreed. "It is quite uncanny. And there were so many 'enemies'. Working at NATO, you knew the intelligence services had you on their radar. It was a really uncomfortable feeling. When the Soviets invaded Afghanistan in the early eighties, tensions ran really high and I wondered if someone was listening in on my phone conversations or whether I was being followed or whether someone might have planted a bomb under my car. I worried whenever I approached a so-called 'critical building'. We had to take a lot a care about where we drove, where to park, and locking our vehicles. Sometimes the security people would check if you had locked your car properly, and, if you hadn't, you could get a security reprimand. And I wasn't even a decision-maker. They were dangerous times. I remember someone driving off from the carpark and leaving their briefcase behind on the ground. It was immediately deemed suspicious and the security boss ordered one of the guards to shoot it. The bullet bounced off the tarmac and punctured the petrol tank of a very nice Mercedes parked nearby. There was a lot of nervousness when those sorts of situations arose."

"What is it like inside NATO?"

"It's a politico-military alliance, not an army. But it was very hierarchical, full of military personnel and we worked very closely with the Supreme Headquarters Allied Powers Europe – SHAPE. My equivalent rank was colonel, and if war had broken out, I would have been issued with a uniform and become a military officer. The hierarchy enabled the organisation to mobilise very quickly."

I was aghast. "But you had no military training?"

"No, I didn't. But in the event of a war, the organisation would be run under military, not civilian, law, and I would have received orders like any other soldier and been subject to the same harsh punishments for not obeying them."

"How did that feel?"

In my mind's eye, I saw an upper-class gentleman with a white moustache wearing full dress uniform, marching around with pips on his shoulder, side-stripes down his trousers and carrying a baton, like in films from another era.

"It didn't bother me much because it seemed so unreal; I didn't sense there was any imminent danger of a war. And if there was, I would be in a bunker somewhere interpreting. There was more hawkish language than there were aggressive acts, although there were some nasty times when Soviet tanks rolled along the other side of the Iron Curtain. I think the Soviets were discerning enough to keep events under control."

I too had lived through the tension of those years. When I first arrived in West-Berlin, the city was like an island of Western capitalism inside communist East Germany. Occupied by Allied forces since the end of the Second World War, and separated from East Berlin and the rest of the German Democratic Republic by the

Berlin Wall – a system of concrete barriers, watchtowers and a no-man's land in the middle known as the 'death strip' – I encountered military vehicles patrolling the streets on a regular basis. Armed police, Allied soldiers in uniform and military helicopters were part of everyday life. My German boyfriend Robert, a photographer, who as a child witnessed the Wall go up, liked to spend his Sunday afternoons taking pictures of it while East German border guards photographed him photographing them. I hated accompanying him.

Whenever friends from the UK visited me, they always wanted to see East Berlin and I did not enjoy taking them. First there were queues at the crossing point at Friedrichstrasse, then you needed to obtain a 24-hour visa, then make a compulsory currency exchange (25 Deutschmarks into overvalued 25 East German marks), which we tried our damnedest to spend in one day and rarely succeeded. There was little of interest for us to buy. And when you did enter East Berlin, I felt a subtle but constant hum of fear talking to people in case they were undercover Stasi (secret police) employees, although everyone I met was pleasant enough. They used the informal, second-person 'du' with ease, loved discussing philosophy, literature, history, music, and were desperate to travel the world. East Germans spoke differently depending on whether they were in public or in private. I only really understood the difference after the Wall came down. And it pained me that I could leave at the end of the day and any new East German folk I had met could not.

Godfrey listened, intrigued, recognising the atmosphere of angst I described.

"And what were the people like who you interpreted for?" I asked.

"Just the same as anywhere else. Some were very open and willing to form a relationship with me, their interpreter, and there were also others where I got the impression that I was seen as a talking robot. They had no interest in developing a working relationship with me."

"So how did you get from NATO to NVC?"

"By 1983, I had separated from Rolande and begun another relationship. We had had five children and in our separation agreement, I had kept too little money for myself. My NATO bosses became concerned, informed the British authorities and in a special security conversation that followed, I realised they were worried about my finances and that I might be vulnerable to bribes. A few days later, I was asked to leave the building immediately and not return. I was given three hours to collect my belongings and see some colleagues and told that I could make my defence once I was gone. I did, and received a lot of support from the Staff Association."

"Jeez."

"It's funny actually. I had a farewell party and someone from the NATO administration came and asked me if I would come back as a trainer to help with internal conflicts, which obviously exist, just as they do in any organisation, so that's the link to NVC."

Godfrey continued: "NATO is about maintaining peace, avoiding World War Three. And that is very similar to my present work, except in NVC I take the approach that we are human beings and if we can talk with each other, we can understand each other." He paused for a second. "To a certain extent that was also going on at NATO, especially in the Outreach Programmes, which began after the Berlin Wall came down. People from Eastern European countries were invited to attend NATO meetings as observers and we started seeing Russian uniforms walking around the building. That was strange, but the atmosphere was definitely welcoming. They were signs of a new beginning. We did a lot of work around preventative communication, meaning rather than wait until there is a threat of war, you engage in dialogue, listen, learn to communicate constructively. The idea is that then, we might not want to go to war with each other. I enjoyed that."

The fall of the Berlin Wall in early November 1989 marked a new beginning not only for NATO. Then, I had lived close to Checkpoint Charlie, the East-West crossing for Allied personnel and foreigners and a flashpoint during the Cold War. The Thursday night when East Germany announced that its citizens could move freely between East and West, Robert and I rushed out to the checkpoint to celebrate and welcome East Berliners to the West. The energy and excitement in the city were tangible. It was one huge party that lasted for weeks. West Berliners were free to explore the surrounding countryside and East Berliners could travel freely and shop in West Berlin.

The reunification of Germany that followed prompted a boom in training programmes. Communication trainers, like myself, were in high demand. Initially, the surprise and relief at the peaceful nature of the transition was huge. Two years later, a new vocabulary suggested the joy of reunification was waning. Terms like 'Besser-Wessi' meaning smartass from the West, and 'Mecker-Ossi', describing East Germans as constant complainers, became buzzwords. The rift between regions became more apparent. Calls for the return of the Wall could be heard from both sides.

It took a new generation for things to settle into a sense of shared community, Berlin as one single city, and many transformative events helped along the way. Berlin became the new capital of a reunified Germany, there was massive reconstruction and infrastructure refurbishment, and, with the arrival of the digital age, everyone was united in facing accelerating change.

Godfrey chuckled to himself.

"What?"

"In the men's toilets at NATO there was a small mirror in front of every basin. From the urinals you could see between the mirrors into the cubicles if the cubicle door was open. I remember going to the loo and caught sight of a man in one of the cubicles having a pee. He kept turning around, watching his back and peeing all over the place. He was on such high alert that he couldn't close the door or look where he was aiming."

"Or maybe he was taking pleasure in peeing all over NATO!" I suggested, laughing, reflecting that Godfrey was quite a precious cargo. I so enjoyed our chats, the skipping back and forth from factual, historical stories to witty personal anecdotes.

"When did you work at the UN?"

"In the mid-eighties interpreting Spanish into English as a freelancer. It was highly technical stuff about agriculture. Many years later, a participant in one of my NVC courses working with the G8 group at the UN on climate change wanted to incorporate NVC into the daily workings of the UN."

"I can't imagine that was easy, Godfrey. How is NVC received in these big organisations?" I was curious to know if his experience matched mine. Over the past ten years, interest in NVC has spiralled, especially in companies that are restructuring, employing change management, looking to hire younger employees, or start-ups run by youthful entrepreneurs. However, traditionally structured organisations are often slow to embrace ideas that could threaten what NVC practitioners would call 'domination culture'.

I first learned about 'domination culture' paradigms and the alternative concept of 'power-with' in a workshop with Marshall Rosenberg. It has fascinated me ever since, encouraging me to find ways of working and living together in which everyone exists on eye-level and decisions are made by finding agreement or consent. In NVC, consent means a group arrives at a decision by integrating diverse perspectives and finding the highest level of unanimity possible. It is a real alternative to majority rule and is very different to the traditional trickle-down power structure of most organisations. I found it exhilarating when put into practice.

Godfrey considered his answer carefully.

"It goes two ways. In one sense, NVC is poorly received in a 'power-over' structure, where bosses believe that people have to obey them. But in organisations like the European Commission, where I still conduct trainings, as well as big and smaller businesses, the degree of employee autonomy is indeed growing. It is becoming more a question of 'power-with' rather than 'power-over'. The old story of obedience and allegiance is changing and moving closer to connecting with peoples' hearts instead of playing to their fears.

At the Commission, I don't talk about Nonviolent Communication because it sounds like a hangover from 1968; they wouldn't like that. I've changed the title of my training to 'Needs-based Communication'; but of course, it is based on the spirit of NVC. Whenever I offer stress management, time management, team building, or the art of living, the ideas that I'm using are absolutely based on needs. Participants recognise the concepts of self-judgements or that they criticise each other and argue, and then, starting from those examples, I always focus on needs, universal needs."

Godfrey yawned.

"Take forty winks," I told him, but he had already nodded off.

I first learned about NVC from colleagues who described it as a set of mediation tools. Then, when I met Marshall for the first time, I realised there was much more to it than that. He embodied such an empathic spirit that it went straight to the heart of everyone he spoke with. The focus on needs driving every behaviour is the central element in NVC and creates connection like no other model I have encountered. It is in our choice of strategies, the way we seek to get our needs met, that we differ.

As we neared Paris, I signalled to take the slip road to the Aire de Resson-Ouest and pulled into the carpark, finding a spot among the other cars, lorries, families and motorhomes, who like us, needed to take a break from motorway driving.

Godfrey woke with a start as always. Outside, he strolled over to the playground area where he found a line of wooden stumps set at different heights. He began hopping along them watched by some curious children. I poured us some tea from my flask.

He sat down beside me slightly breathless. "I feel lighter!"

"That looked fun!" I passed him a cup. I considered whether I could manage jumping around like that. My body was still sore and achy, but I had not needed any painkillers on the journey so far. I remained seated. I didn't want to push my luck and also had my eye on the clock.

Godfrey took a sip and seemed keen to tell me something he had remembered. "People get the wrong idea sometimes about military folk. We think they are hard and heartless, but my time at NATO taught me that is not the case. I remember a wonderful man, a member of the West German military staff, seconded to NATO, who was in charge of a committee that the political wing consulted when they wanted military advice. When you were in a meeting with him, you knew he never wanted to see a single shot fired anywhere or a single person killed ever. He was anything but trigger-happy and more of a philosopher who wanted real peace in this world."

In that moment, I felt an unexpected surge of pride at having chosen Germany as my home. During my formative years in Berlin, I had been surrounded by peace activists and conscientious objectors. When the Cold War ended, most Germans believed peace would be more or less permanent. I had met so many Germans with an inbuilt wariness towards militarism, war and soldiering, a reflexive reluctance to being drawn onto the battlefield ever again. As a country, foreign military deployments remain tightly restricted and conscription has been abolished. Sensitivity to the impact of war is acute. And in Berlin in particular, the weight of history hangs heavy in the collective memory. With a strange combination of both sadness and joy still swirling in my head, we strolled back to the car, ready for the next leg of our journey.

Country walk with Bo

Godfrey as a schoolboy

Godfrey in first roleplay with Grandma Dorothy

Hugh, Sabina and Godfrey (l-r)

Moving back to Belgium

On the road to Wales

Sabina and Godfrey on horseback

Spencer family photo (l-r Godfrey with dog Dilly-Hugh and William-Sabina-Mother with Thomas-Manuela-Mary)

Spencer parents Johanna + Michael wedding

Tea break in France

The Butte de Lion

Thomas and William Spencer

CHAPTER 7

INTRODUCING MARSHALL

Godfrey and I arrived on Aileen's doorstep, dripping wet and out of breath having dashed – once again – from the car to avoid a storm. Aileen opened the front door and I could see her husband Fred and his mother, known to all as Maman, waiting to greet us in the hallway of their cosy fifteenth-century house. To my huge embarrassment, Godfrey, who had never met my friends before, walked past them, dumped his bag on the floor and asked where his room was, as if he was arriving at a hotel. I could see a look of consternation cross Aileen's face. A sticky situation.

The tension didn't last long as Aileen and Maman embraced me and Fred called out to Godfrey, "See you in the morning!"

Godfrey stopped in his tracks, realising where he was and followed us into the dining room looking quite fatigued. Soon, Fred opened a bottle of excellent chablis. Godfrey and Aileen, who had worked as English-French interpreters for people in high political office, started talking shop, while Maman served beautifully decorated hors d'oeuvres, baked ricotta, lotte à l'armoricaine and tarte tatin, delicious traditional Brittany fair. Talking and laughing, we spent a delightful evening together.

Introducing Marshall

As Godfrey and I ascended the circular staircase to the guest rooms on the top floor of the turret, I teased him about our arrival in pretend admonishment. Hearing my list of observations about those first moments, Godfrey looked quite sheepish, almost ashamed, and put his hand to his mouth, shaking his head. I had understood quickly what had happened. He had been chatting with me in the car, was probably all talked out and was so used to arriving at hotels after travelling that his instincts had taken over. I reassured him that there was no lasting damage, no need to bring it up again in the morning or apologise. I did overhear him telling Maman the next day how confused he gets with all his travelling, not always knowing quite where he is. She nodded, smiling at him as she handed over a plate of fresh warm buns for breakfast.

We set off early after saying our goodbyes, a flask of peppermint tea in my hand. We had enjoyed a lovely visit. Aileen and Fred still ask after Godfrey's health to this day.

The French countryside rolled by, open and flat and there was not a cloud in the sky, yet.

"You know, Godfrey, I've never asked you. How did you meet Marshall?"

Sitting comfortably in the passenger seat, he began: "I had a colleague at the University of Louvain's interpreters' school who had a friend who was an NVC trainer. They were both very enthusiastic about Marshall. My colleague said, 'There is someone you just have to meet; he has a message for you.' That pricked my curiosity. I didn't know anything about this Marshall Rosenberg or NVC when I travelled to Paris to attend my first training session in 1997. I enjoyed it tremendously, although at the time, I didn't really understand why. So, I attended another training as soon as I could, three months later, in La Rochelle."

That triggered a thought. I checked our route with Madame SatNav.

"Do you want to go there, to La Rochelle? It's not far off our route. We could have lunch and stretch our legs with a stroll along the harbour?"

Godfrey nodded with a huge smile on his face.

"So, what happened at the course there?"

I had met Marshall for the first time in 1998 in Berlin while training to become a mediator and had no idea that Godfrey and I had come to NVC around the same time.

"There were eighteen of us, plus interpreters. Marshall suggested we take a look at anger. I volunteered to do a role-play with him. I described to Marshall how my father spoke when he was furious, how he shouted and ranted close to my face. I used to fear for my life although he never touched me. Marshall became my father and I became my six-year-old self. Marshall insulted me just as my father would: 'You useless little bastard, what the hell do you think you're doing? Give me that spanner!'"

When I heard Godfrey tell this story I was surprised. At that time, I hadn't seen Marshall slip into a role and copy the behaviour of a perpetrator before. Typically, he would simply stand in and listen empathically. I learned later of the term 'role-play by proxy', where a trainer/counsellor takes on the role of an absent person when working with a client. In this, Marshall's particular skill was to support the participant to air their pain and anger safely while he spoke from the heart about what the absent person had done. I wondered if he had sensed that Godfrey would be able to cope with this rather different and provocative teaching style.

"What happened next?"

"Marshall asked me how I felt when he said these things to me. In a split second, I'd crossed my arms over my chest and proclaimed that I didn't have any feelings. 'First of all, I'm a man and secondly, I'm English, and we just don't have feelings!'

Marshall said, 'That's very interesting.' And then he started making empathic guesses about the pain that I was probably feeling when my father was in one of his rages. He guessed my need for consideration, for gentleness, for unconditional love, for dignity. In less than five minutes, I was sobbing my eyes out. I looked up through my tears and saw twenty other people also with tears streaming down their faces. I thought to myself, 'You know what Godfrey, maybe you do have feelings.'" He chuckled.

I had heard Godfrey say this before in his workshops, which always made people laugh, because it was so in contrast to how he is now: very willing to express his feelings and vulnerability publicly, shedding tears at the drop of a hat.

"Then what happened?"

"I relaxed, and he began speaking as my father about his own needs when he was angry and shouting. I can guess now, although I don't recall Marshall's exact words, that they were likely to be needs for safety, for support, and to get things done, for accomplishment."

Godfrey took a deep breath. "It was so powerful, Marshall's empathy. I remember bursting into more floods of tears because it was so fast, spot-on, and true: such good guesses. I instantly knew there was something very important happening, and it was also mysterious. I was both very upset and comforted, very interested too – all at the same time. I think from that moment, when Marshall role-played my father, I never looked back. I wanted to discover more about his method, his way of healing and teaching; the desire to learn and understand the process kindled something in me. There was definitely a message in it for me that was bigger than anything else I had ever received in my life. And I decided to go to as many NVC trainings as I could."

I completely understood what Godfrey meant. Watching Marshall work with his calm, gentle way of creating connection, was magical. No sleight of hand, no showiness, no hidden tricks or agenda, quite simply listening and speaking to the person in front of him with honest and open empathy.

Godfrey smiled and dabbed his eyes. "And I've been crying ever since! Actually, it's what Marshall recommends: that we cry all of our tears, of sadness, of anger and of joy."

Of all the different self-development methods and approaches I learned and practised during my formative years studying psychology in Berlin, NVC brought me closest to my most painful, private experiences and supported a depth of healing that felt very empowering. I am not one to cry easily, but having a safe place to weep and show my hidden emotions just made sense to me. NVC tied together many strands of what I had learned so far. I loved that it was based on a simple understanding of how human connection functions: to listen intently and guess what is going on for someone under the surface. I felt that Marshall embodied an age-old wisdom.

I realised I had been lost in thought as Godfrey wept quietly beside me, so I pulled in for a short break and a cup of tea. Godfrey wanted to reflect further on his first experience with Marshall, but was a bit stuck for words.

I broke the silence. "When Marshall guessed that were you scared because you needed to feel safe and be reassured you were not going to die at that moment, did you feel a sense of relief that someone finally understood you?"

He nodded and sniffed. "That's exactly it!"

Back on the road, a little further along the A87 toward the coast, Godfrey started talking about another remarkable role-play he'd witnessed.

"It was during a training in the US around Easter in 1998. The woman was about thirty-five and her father, a policeman, had sexually abused her from the age of five."

I inhaled loudly and held my breath for a few seconds, and whispered "Jeez."

Godfrey looked over and we caught each other's gaze. I'd heard many stories begin like this during my time in social work, but they never failed to shock. I nodded to him, signalling that I was ready to hear some more.

"I still remember her screaming at Marshall, who was taking the place of her father in the session. He encouraged her to say everything she wanted to say. Marshall listened empathically to her words, staying with her pain in that very moment. Through her tears, she shouted, 'I can still remember the things you made me do, the pain, I was suffocating. And somehow, I felt it was my fault, that was almost the worst part.'

After about an hour of the role-play, there was a lot of tension in the room, a lot of people in tears. Marshall asked 'Is there anything else you'd like to tell me?' She replied, 'Not for the moment.'

Then, still in the role of the father, he asked, 'Would you be willing for me to tell you what I was experiencing at the times I was having sex with you?' And she said, 'Yes'.

As the father, Marshall talked about his need for warmth, intimacy, belonging – all sorts of beautiful universal needs although he chose to do these horrendous things with his very small daughter."

I thought about the many trainings I had participated in where I witnessed Marshall work with similar issues around trauma and abuse. Despite hearing the clear relief felt by the person he worked with at finally being heard, every time after those sessions, I've also listened to the anguish of the observers in the participant group. Their upset was not just a compassionate response to someone else's pain, but also a concern around accountability. Marshall had an amazing capacity to feel into the perpetrator's heart and soul and offer insight into their behaviour and their humanness. It could be disconcerting to witness as he empathised with a person who had hurt another, guessing at their needs. But in doing so, he wasn't agreeing with their behaviour or choices or offering excuses; he was trying to give the survivor the opportunity to understand what had happened to them and take a step further in their healing. But this can be misunderstood.

"I think there is a danger that people say 'what about the abuse?', and think Marshall was inviting her to understand her perpetrator, empathise and move on," I interrupted Godfrey, playing devil's advocate. "Like empathy gets the father off the hook!"

"No, and this is really important. When Marshall talked about the needs of those who commit atrocious acts that others pay for, such as child abuse, rape, murder, he was not in any way condoning those acts. Just because you want something, it doesn't mean you can take it, or there is any obligation for anyone else to fulfil your needs. Marshall suggested that there is only really one moral law: to be aware of the consequences of our acts and take responsibility for them. When I witnessed this role-play, never for a minute did I perceive Marshall as approving the father's behaviour. He was demonstrating that every human being shares the same deep needs. Then it's up to you how you behave, meaning those needs are not attached to any specific strategy.

What I saw in that role-play was that Marshall was connected to the very deepest aspects of life in that father, which are totally beyond anything he had decided to do to his daughter."

I nodded. "I had never seen anyone do this kind of work with victims of violence until I met Marshall. When I became a counsellor, I noticed there is a point in the victim's recovery or healing process when they make a shift from judging the offender and instead, start to want to understand how someone could commit that violence and why they were chosen as the victim. In my experience, this really helps."

Around the same time as my first workshop with Marshall in Berlin learning about NVC, courts began to use mediation in high-profile cases, and I became fascinated by it. I read about systemic violence and began to understand the structural patterns of violence I had witnessed in my childhood.

Godfrey jumped in, eager to follow my train of thought. "We have to realise that every behaviour is based on a desire to meet our needs. I may well flout another's needs by choosing a strategy that hurts someone else. If we, however, follow the focus of everyone's needs getting met and broaden our array of choices, then we can co-create a world of non-violence, where we encourage each other to make acceptable and life-serving choices."

"So how did the workshop end?"

"The woman gave feedback to the group the next day and remarked that she had never been listened to like that before and it had been really healing. Marshall, as her father, had given her his full attention, taken on board all the pain, given her space to express it without judgement, cynicism or deflection. I have no contact with her now and do not know whether the healing was complete, probably not at once. What I can say is that she made a major breakthrough in her life." He paused, apparently reflecting on what had been an intense learning experience.

"I totally believe that," I said. "After my studies, when I first encountered NVC, it really hit me that if it were possible to leave the paradigm of blame, shame and punishment, we could facilitate moving beyond the system of violence. When people who commit violence feel others see their humanity, real change can happen. I've seen it. People become remorseful. For those that have been violated, they achieve a kind of inner peace when they see the other as a human being, and feel seen themselves. I think that was what Marshall really understood."

"Indeed. The thing is, healing does not happen if we get stuck in anger, even if it is justified. It perpetuates fear and hatred. The hatred produces violence both inside and outside. Empathy connects across the hatred, takes us along the road to forgiveness. Nothing is unforgivable. It is better for us humans to be in the place of forgiveness. I believe it was Alice Herz-Sommer, a Holocaust survivor, who said in an interview, 'Hatred gnaws at the heart of the person who hates.'"

I sighed. Not only was Marshall's skill set and understanding of the human spirit a quantum leap away from the norm and carried the potential to overturn structural violence, NVC, with its focus on universal needs, was also open to being easily misunderstood.

Godfrey appeared to read my mind. "The misunderstanding may be around the word forgiveness, which is sometimes understood in this way: 'The act you committed was fine, I forgive you.'"

"I don't use the word forgiveness like that."

"To me, forgiveness is about understanding the very deep reasons that led someone to commit that crime. And I truly believe the world becomes a safer place if a criminal is listened to, and, by giving everyone the opportunity to be listened to deeply without judgement in that moment."

He added quickly, "Don't get me wrong, I don't want anyone to be unprotected. And there should be places for people who are a danger to society to live away from society, for the safety of others. I'm simply asking that in our interactions with those who have committed abusive acts towards others, we see their distress rather than their wickedness. Rumi, the poet, said something I agree with: 'There is a field beyond right-doing and wrong-doing. I'll meet you there.' It's the only place we can truly meet. It helps me if I can see what is in the deepest recesses of a person's heart when they commit an act that I find reprehensible, and not get stuck in right and wrong."

I agreed but could also see that in the face of atrocious crimes, this idea might be hard for society at large to swallow.

"Have you heard of Leymah Gbowee?" I asked.

Godfrey shook his head.

"She's a Liberian peace activist. In Africa there's the concept of 'ubuntu' or shared humanity. Her interpretation is, 'I am because of who we all are', which speaks to the fact that we are all connected and that one can only grow and progress through the growth and progression of others."

"That sounds similar to the concept of 'restorative circles', much used by Dominic Barter in his work in the favelas in Brazil."

My eyes widened. "Ah, I went to his training session when he came to Berlin. He's another British expat. We get everywhere!"

We drove on in silence for a while, letting the conversation settle and taking in the beauty of the Parc Naturel Régional du Marais Poitevin with its lush vineyards and pine trees, when I spotted the sign for La Rochelle. We were about half an hour away from lunch and I was sure Godfrey would also welcome a break. I certainly needed one. I wound down the window and took a long breath of cool fresh air feeling it wash over my face and bring me back to the present moment.

Arriving in Montolieu

Berlin 2015

Berlin lakeside with Toni the poodle

Dinner in Le Mans

Godfrey and Klaus on the morning "workout" in Montolieu

Godfrey with "gun" in Frankfurt bookstore

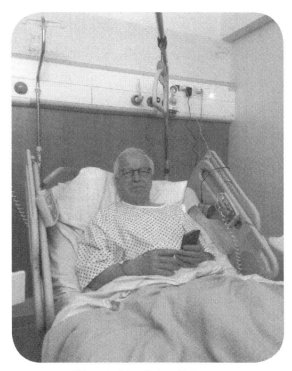

Hospital in Saint Etienne

Midnight arrival in Montolieu

Sunset in Montolieu

The chariot

CHAPTER 8

EMPATHIC INTERPRETATION

A s we approached the outskirts of La Rochelle, I could smell the moist, spicy air, laced with the saltiness of the Atlantic Ocean. It fired my appetite. I needed food, having missed out on the buns for breakfast. I navigated the city's complicated one-way system, eventually finding the carpark at the Place de Verdun, right in the centre of the old town. We tumbled out of the car, ready to stretch our legs, and strolled through a large square surrounded by handsome Renaissance-era buildings, past rows of tall eighteenth-century apartment blocks with iron balconies and red-tiled roofs, admiring the outside of the St Louis Cathedral, and headed towards the ancient port, marvelling at half-timbered medieval buildings dotted about.

"What was Marshall like to interpret for?"

I was interested in Godfrey's take on him as a person. From the late nineties, with my friend Andrea who employed me as a trainer at her Institute for Mediation, I had been involved in organising Marshall's annual February visits to Berlin when he would attend our yearly training for business mediators. His presence was the highlight of the event. He captivated everyone. Lunch with him and his translator Sven was like being backstage with a comedy duo. I think I left more food on my plate than went in to my mouth as their quick, dry humour kept me giggling.

"It was fun to work for Marshall as an interpreter," Godfrey confirmed. "It must have been three months after the training in the US that I attended an International Intensive Training back in France and began interpreting for Marshall, English/French/English, in his workshops. That was the beginning of a long relationship with him. I attended nearly every training he gave in French-speaking countries – Belgium, Switzerland, France, and even in Hungary. That was very fulfilling. I just followed him around."

"Was it difficult to work in a training setting?"

"When I interpret for someone, it feels as if I become part of them, that the connection between us in that moment means I'm not listening to the words but the meaning. With Marshall, I listened to his emotional state as much as his words. If Marshall was moved by what he was saying, I was moved in the same way. When he was in pain or when he was joyful, so was I. All of the depth that Marshall expressed, I expressed too. Because, at that time, we were so close emotionally, intellectually, I could speak immediately after Marshall expressed something, without waiting for another sentence or for him to finish. We synchronised and it was very fulfilling. I think people were very aware of the synergy between us. People listening often said they were not aware that I was there. Although I do remember that there were tricky situations. One time, at a training in Italy, I was working as a trainer and an interpreter, combining both roles. In the end, it was very overwhelming, for me and the participants. It was confusing for them as they associated my voice with the interpreter, even when I was the trainer."

"How did you become a trainer?"

We arrived at the old port with its two stone towers guarding its sea entrance.

"The more trainings I took part in, the closer I got to Marshall. After about three years of interpreting for him, I mentioned that I would like to work towards certification, as a CNVC [Center for Nonviolent Communication] trainer. He simply replied, 'You're certified'. Looking back, I am a little sad about that, that I missed the detailed certification process there is nowadays. I too would have liked three or more years of learning, feedback, group processes, with all the work on the concept, didactics and personal learning issues."

Finding a spot in a quiet brasserie on the quayside, we ordered a seafood lunch and took a moment to relax, watching the sunshine dancing off the surface of the water. Sailing boats glided in and out to sea. I could have stayed there all day and would have loved to have taken a drive out to the salt marshes and villages of the Île de Ré, but there wasn't time.

Having co-founded the German NVC organisation, DACH, I knew many trainers who had found the certification process daunting, exhausting and hard work. For me it was an enriching experience and I'm glad I took my time with it. Godfrey had definitely missed out.

"Why do you think Marshall was confident to certify you as a trainer just like that?"

"I don't think he thought that I had any tremendous skills; he saw that I had a big heart, that I have room for other people in it. After about a year of working as a trainer with him, I faced a big decision: should I reduce my hours further – I'd been reinstated at

NATO by then – to work both as a trainer and consultant for NVC or leave my job entirely? It was a major turning point. I realised that working in NVC was so important to me that it justified risking everything."

"What inspired you? It can't have been money?"

"No, it wasn't money. It was the reception Marshall got everywhere. And I experienced that myself. Something grew in me, something in the nature of trust: trust that I could contribute and that people could benefit by seeing what deep clarity and honesty means and by being the recipients of empathy. I became a member of the Board of CNVC and was in contact with the spirit of NVC every day. I started to get known locally as a trainer and noticed in all my work that people were reacting very differently to me compared to when I was an interpreter. There was something like a special welcome that was very touching."

"And how were things with your family? Did that change?"

"It's strange. I would have thought I'd have seen the impact first in my family, but I was holding back somehow. I didn't want to impose these new ideas on anybody. When I think back to my family relationships, I wasn't able to bring in that consciousness and many things stayed tense, hostile, difficult. It's only now that my general attitude, the way that I am with my family, has changed, and I feel more welcome there too."

"What was it like working so closely with Marshall as a trainer?"

I had relished my own contact with him in Berlin, chauffeuring him around and hosting his workshops. He was a joy, a great storyteller and easy to be around. I felt I got to know the 'secret' Marshall that not many people had access to. Born to Jewish parents, he told me that his birth name was Moishe. His mother and father had changed it to Marshall around the time of the race riots in Detroit, his home town, in the forties. He was bullied in school and they feared for his safety. But it had never occurred to me to want to work with him. He came across as a solitary operator. But perhaps I was wrong.

"One of the wonderful things about working with him was that he took the time with us as a team at the end of every day to celebrate and mourn everything that had been happening. It was like a daily ritual of reflection that Marshall encouraged, that kept you focussed on the here and now, in touch with your inner state of being and it supported connection in the group. It didn't take very long because I don't think he had much energy left after working all day. He would show his vulnerability and encourage us to show ours. In my experience he very rarely lost sight of what was going on in himself and what was going on with others."

"How was he vulnerable?"

"I'll give you an example that shocked me at the time because I didn't understand what was happening. We were at a training in the US, my first IIT, and there was a man there who wanted to be an assistant trainer with Marshall. This man had written a book that was not well received by the NVC community; he received a lot of criticism from some main players on the trainer scene who said that it wasn't NVC. Marshall said to him, 'If that's the way you work, behave and see NVC, then I don't want to work with you.'

It was perfectly clear, legitimate, but I felt uncomfortable at the way he said it in front of fifty people. The man was so full of goodwill and energy. Marshall's reaction stumped me a little. I asked myself, how can a man of peace with a great love for people say something so cruel to a potential trainer? It didn't seem necessary, healthy or kind. It would have been easy for Marshall to change the subject but instead he went for the potential confrontation. I now understand that he was showing who he was, expressing his honesty, without judgement."

"How did the man respond?"

"I believe he understood that there was something still evolving in his own learning. He's a successful trainer now." Godfrey continued. "And there were other occasions. At a Board meeting in Mexico, Marshall said some harsh things about a former friend who had forwarded a confidential email that he had received from Marshall to other people. Marshall was angry, hurt, abrupt, upset – he put frankness ahead of niceness. Another time, at a training in Belgium someone asked Marshall to demonstrate how he would give empathy to George W. Bush in a role-play. This was in the run up to the Iraq War. He refused, saying that he was so triggered by Bush junior that he couldn't possibly do that. The room went silent."

"How did this influence how you saw Marshall as a person? How you liked him?"

"I liked him as a person, absolutely, except when he said things that made me squirm."

"Like what?"

"I was in a car with him once being driven from the airport to a training venue. Listening to the organiser describe where he was going to sleep, Marshall realised that there was no en suite washing facilities. Marshall stated: 'I'm not staying there; it's below my threshold of tolerance. Would you find me a hotel?' I was not interpreting for him but still felt uncomfortable. There was no negotiation. I admired his clarity about what was not acceptable to him. After all, his accommodation requirements had been put in writing. But he seemed impatient, tired, and it was hard for me to hear him speak that way. The message I and the organiser heard was 'You've done a bad job'. Although, that wasn't what he said, I could see the organiser wilting, devastated."

"No empathy from Marshall?"

"Not for one second. I realised Marshall was a human being like all of us; when he got upset, he might not be able to stay with the process. Marshall would have said he was just being completely honest and that how the other person receives his statement was their responsibility. I still think he could have expressed himself differently. But Marshall was straight to the point. Now we'd call that 'scary honesty'."

"Did he ever say anything to you that was really hard to hear?"

"Yes. I went up to him after a particularly long day to tell him how much I had enjoyed the session and how wonderful he was, and he said simply, 'That doesn't help me at all'. He asked for concrete observations of things he had done or said during the session, and what needs had been met in me."

Our starters, steaming bowls of soupe de poissons Rochelaise arrived. As I spooned the delicious medley of rock fish, carrots, tomatoes, celery, leeks and garlic laced with Cognac into my mouth, I recalled Marshall asking for feedback from our trainee mediators in Berlin, making it clear that this was also an exercise in changing praise into concrete observations. He really walked his talk as a teacher.

"What drove Marshall on do you think?" I asked. "His schedule was crazy."

Godfrey nodded. "I heard someone criticise his schedule once and he replied, 'When you see the way I am received everywhere, how can I do anything else?'" He dabbed his eyes with his napkin and stopped speaking for a moment. "People responded to him with such admiration and love. He was so important to people. When he heard someone had requested a training or a conference, he always wanted to say yes. He kept such a punishing schedule, but he knew the choices he was making. He wanted to get the message of Nonviolent Communication out as broadly and deeply as it would go, so that as many people as possible could have an opportunity to create a different world, where human beings, instead of thinking in terms of right and wrong, would begin thinking of what needs are met or unmet."

The breeze tickled my face. "Your experience working with Marshall sounds intense."

"Working for him as an interpreter, I never sensed even a hint of criticism or impatience. It was a joy to work for him because he had a tremendous sense of humour. One of the difficulties was that when the sessions were over, he was very reserved. Very often he would eat on his own, or, if we ate with him, he would be quiet, although those around him often wanted to chat and learn more. I do remember one role-play in which I was the husband and Marshall played my wife, which I didn't get anything from. I thought, well, this one didn't work. It was good though, because it made Marshall into a human being instead of an empathy god. I enjoyed that side of him. And when his girlfriend once said to him at a workshop, 'Marshall you're the worst jackal on the face of the Earth!', I thought that was so wonderful to hear and I felt so very much less lonely!"

Godfrey laughed and began to eat.

Marshall used the term 'jackal' to describe the use of judgemental words. On a long car journey with a colleague who was complaining to him about her husband, Marshall had asked her, "What makes you want to stay with this jackal?" And she replied: "That's exactly the right word to describe him, Marshall!"

They began using it in trainings to denote a person seeking power over someone else because they were not in touch with their fear and instead acted like a bully. Marshall was already using the term 'duck energy' to symbolise empathic communication, which he came up with after watching his grandchildren joyously feeding ducks. The idea was that in giving empathy, we are also feeding ourselves. This symbol changed later to a giraffe after some Swedish TV producers suggested to Marshall, who was being interviewed, that his duck puppet didn't work on TV. Marshall reportedly chose a giraffe instead because of its big heart.

The waiter opened the sunshades.

"Marshall had many girlfriends all over the world." Godfrey finished his soup.

I raised my eyebrows. "Really?"

"Didn't you know?" He sounded surprised. "And he had relationships with many women students during his trainings."

I almost dropped my spoon. I never saw him acting inappropriately toward any female participant or trainer during his visits to Berlin. If I had, I would have been disturbed and concerned for our students and it would have undermined my faith in his teachings. I was really clear about professional ethical standards. A profound disquiet crept over me. In that moment, when Marshall wasn't there to explain himself, my memories of him had been sullied.

"Wow. I remember on his visits to Berlin thinking he sometimes looked like just an old guy with a guitar and some raggedy puppets.

But he created such a magical atmosphere that participant numbers grew every year. Why did you keep going to his workshops, if you knew about this?"

I was shocked but I couldn't imagine Marshall ever being pushy or a predator. I looked at Godfrey to see if he understood my distress.

"Because they were so thrilling, so intense; they involved so much learning, so much hope for a new Godfrey to enter into the world, receive support for myself and support other people. His humility was very attractive. He didn't ever put himself across as being 'the one who knows'. Instead, it was as if he was inviting you to join him in his experiment with communication. He didn't listen to peoples' words; he heard what was underneath, what made people tick, what was alive in the deepest part of them, what was behind their behaviour. That inspired me. His mixture of great depth and light humour was something that I haven't met in anybody else in the same way. It was so rewarding to be working with a man like that. And I mirrored him: I shifted from translating words to translating what was going on inside someone."

The waiter cleared our plates and brought our main course. I took a long sip of my glass of water.

Godfrey's tone turned sad. "As Marshall got older, before he got married again and settled in Albuquerque for good, I realised how exhausted he was. He gave his life for humanity and I feel quite upset about that. He rarely took holidays. I remember after one training in Hungary about a decade ago, I flew home to rest but Marshall flew off to work somewhere. We met a few days later in Bordeaux for a training. I'd received a request for him to fit in an extra conference on the day in addition to the planned evening session and I passed the request on to his scheduler who had instructions to accept. So, he flew in, gave one conference in the late afternoon, which went on longer than expected, then gave another that evening that stretched on into the night. He got up at the crack of dawn the next morning to fly to Sweden to speak at another conference at 9:00 a.m. To me, that's a person who is totally unable to care for himself. I think, towards the end of his life, with his Alzheimer's, it was almost like his body telling him to let go."

I waved my hand in front of Godfrey's face to get his attention. "That reminds me of someone – the lack of self-care, forgetting his needs, forgetting to eat sometimes …."

Godfrey mumbled something about not learning his lesson from his sarcoma. I looked at him with mock opprobrium. A life-threatening cancer in his back had failed to slow him down. We made a pact for the upcoming retreat. We were to meet every day for thirty minutes, just us, and Godfrey would recount all the ways he had been meeting his needs for self-care. I was to serve as his listener, reminder and 'scolder'. I wasn't sure that I wanted to take on that last role. He reassured me that it would do him the world of good to get his "ass kicked" if he forgot to keep his promises to himself.

It would be interesting, to say the least, to see how that would work out.

CHAPTER 9

THE INTIMACY OF CONFLICT

I was in no rush to leave La Rochelle, but I wanted to keep my promise to Godfrey to get him to Montolieu in time for the trainers' meeting, scheduled for that evening. The course was to begin in two days. Godfrey's childlike quality of being totally in the moment meant he didn't seem too bothered about being on time, but with a five-hour drive ahead of us, I wanted to be there for dinner. As we wandered back to the car, Godfrey called and arranged to meet the trainer team at La Place, a favourite café near the fountain in the village square. He closed the call with his usual, "Bisous!"

While the sea air tugged at me, the hot July sun meant the air-conditioning in the car was beautifully cool on my skin. The afternoon traffic was lighter as we eased through the streets. Many of the restaurants had closed after lunch and the pavements were emptier.

"Lorna, I'm so glad you're driving me." He paused. I smiled. "But I don't want you to take on such a commitment because you feel you have to."

"I love keeping commitments!" I checked Madame SatNav.

Godfrey folded his arms. "For me, they can feel like a constraint."

"But no, they're a driving force. Once I've said yes to something, that's like saying 'yes, I am really going for this relationship. I really want it to work'. In terms of our friendship, keeping a commitment is my way of contributing to a sense of safety between us."

"I love what I'm hearing, Lorna, but I'm also concerned. Imagine a friend responds to your request, says yes in the moment - and remember that moment is the only moment we live in! She senses a great willingness to do whatever it is. But then the next day, water has flowed under the bridge and she finds that her willingness is not there. To me, following through on this self-inflicted 'obligation' is a form of violence."

We had dived right back into a meaty topic. I understood Godfrey's concern about being dictated to and getting stuck. I also thought of a friend who had a habit of begrudgingly agreeing to do things she didn't seem to want to do. Dealing with that was too complicated for me.

"I don't want someone to do something if they don't really want to," I replied. "I don't want to be around that kind of energy and resentment. What I'm saying is, I'd much rather someone say beforehand that they are not sure. Otherwise, if they change their mind, I'll be disappointed and the joy is gone."

Godfrey answered slowly, "What I hear you saying is that you believe in the 'here and now' and that you are confident of your willingness that that will hold through thick and thin. I sense you are annoyed when you are looking forward to something, and it falls through. Then you think the relationship has no substance. Is that right?"

"Absolutely. Commitment for me means the intention, that drive, stays. It's a choice, not an obligation. Instead of saying 'my plans have changed, I am just not coming, and you have to accept that', I can change arrangements in agreement with you. That to me is ensuring the connection."

"If you had said to me 'Godfrey, I can't pick you up in Brussels. I feel ill, or the car has broken down, can you make your way there by train?', I can easily accept that. I am very flexible. But you're saying if a lack of care comes across, that's a statement about our connection, almost as if the person doesn't care?"

"Yes. I have an inner 'glitch' that when someone changes their mind on big things they have agreed to, it's like a cancellation of our connection. Take this last month, working on the book, so many unexpected things happened: my ceiling caved in, my wi-fi disappeared, I nearly got knocked over in the street. All sorts of things can happen that change circumstances, but my general willingness and passion to make this work stays. I'm not talking about flexibility; I can be resilient, I know changes can happen, that's fine. I would rather say no today to something if I thought my willingness or capacity could possibly waver."

"I understand and totally agree." Godfrey nodded.

"Someone could say, I love the idea, but I'm not sure if I have the stamina or willingness to see it through. Then I know where I am at. For me, if I agree to this book project now, I am saying yes wholeheartedly. To you, to the book, to myself, my vision. And that is what commitment is to me."

"What about renegotiating a commitment?"

"Godfrey, if you said to me, 'I would like to renegotiate', I am happy to do that." I thought of the many times in the early days of my sabbatical when he had changed the time of our Skype dates because of collisions with his training projects. "Of course, I too have moments where my energy is low and I feel an urge to cancel at the last minute. But I prefer to be reliable. When I feel committed, I will usually plan in little things that make it easier for me to stick to it. Like with this trip now. We stopped at Aileen's home; that was fun. When we get to the village tonight, we will be having dinner with Louise and the other trainers, fun too. I suppose I build in little motivators that help keep me going."

"Lorna," Godfrey assumed a posh accent as if he was about to make a proclamation. "I'm a direct beneficiary of your loyalty, of your constancy and it makes it very comfortable to experience our friendship."

I knew that underneath his jesting, he was being genuinely affectionate.

We had reached Rochefort and it was time for a toilet break already. Egrets and herons circled in the sky above the salt farms and oyster beds of the Charente estuary. Godfrey sniffed the air as he opened the car door. The smell of the fishmonger's stall a little way up ahead caught on the breeze. I would have loved to have stopped for longer to explore this seafood lovers' heaven, but was still full after our excellent lunch.

Back in the car, we continued discussing commitment, duty and obligation in past relationships. Seafood analogies – being a slippery fish, having a hard shell, smelling rotten and eyes glazing over – had us in stitches.

Godfrey turned in his seat, suddenly serious: "Lorna, you don't find anything limiting in the idea of commitment?"

I considered his question. "Well, it's natural for commitment to waver; life happens when you're not expecting it to. But if someone is in my heart, that helps me keep agreements when I've said yes." I paused. "Godfrey, is my conception of commitment so different from yours?"

"Yes, but I love it. My problem is the word commitment. It is often used to make people feel guilty, force people to do things. Like the word disappointed."

I nodded in recognition. I told Godfrey about the time, when I first started exploring NVC and reading the literature, I found a list of feelings and some were highlighted with a warning. Disappointed was one.

Godfrey continued: "Disappointed is so often used as a criticism of someone."

I understood, but was convinced it was also a valid feeling. "Did I tell you I used to go every week to a salsa nightclub?" I asked. "I had a salsa partner, Heiko, who always arrived at the dance club an hour after me. He couldn't seem to get anywhere at the arranged time. We tried everything. We even phoned each other to agree that we were ready to set off immediately and then I would wait an hour before I left. It didn't help much.

One evening, after a full day of Marshall's training, I waited for Heiko at the salsa club. It was 11:00pm. Sitting there like a wallflower, I became curious about how I was feeling. When he finally arrived, I was so joyful to see him. He was a little confused. His tardiness helped me realise that it is indeed possible to feel disappointment without being resentful."

Godfrey appeared to mull over my story. "Back to commitment. Your interpretation is passion, loyalty, connection."

"And work." I sounded almost peeved and was a little surprised at myself. "I put a lot of work into keeping my joy and willingness going. I know it's my responsibility to uphold that, even if I don't like what you do. I could tell you what you have done that is so awful, but I know that won't be helpful if I am still annoyed and being judgemental. Instead, I get in touch with myself, get my needs met and get myself having fun again."

Godfrey frowned. "In my trainings, it's difficult for me when I talk about loyalty in connection with commitment. I so want to find other reasons to be together than obligation. If I am not in a relationship out of pure willingness, joy, a need to contribute to the other person's well-being, both parties will pay heavily for that. I would be better off being somewhere else."

It sounded like he was referring to something or someone specific. I knew I was being nosey, but asked anyway. "You've seen that in your intimate relationships?"

"Yep. When I first married and moved to Belgium, I got into obligation very quickly. I was part of a church system that dictated that when you got married, you committed for life and you stayed together until death did you part. After nineteen years I couldn't survive in my marriage and wanted out. I remember visiting my parents for their fiftieth wedding anniversary celebration and my father, having drunk a bit, scolded me, 'Couldn't you have made an effort at your marriage like us?' I didn't have time to answer before my younger brother, having drunk some too, answered our father, 'You two should have separated years ago!'

That was very hard for my father to hear. The pain that I experienced as a child was in large part due to the fact that I didn't seem to see much love between my father and mother. As children, I said to myself that we would have been better off if they had lived in different places. It wasn't wise for them to stay together because of commitment."

It crossed my mind that maybe Godfrey's religious education, full of duty, fear and obligation made it incomprehensible, almost alien, to be able to consciously relish and choose commitment in a friendship or intimate relationship. Before I offered him these reflections, he began speaking about parents and children, his voice quite energised.

"I've known two women who both left their children with other carers, moved away and built new lives. No contact whatsoever with their children. I have enormous admiration for them. They left not only for their own good, but for the good of all the people in their immediate orbit. Imagine living with a mother who conveys, without words, that the only reason she is still around is because she has to be, and she's thinking, 'I don't want to be with you; I don't love you and I would much rather be somewhere else, but it is my duty to stay.' My response to that would be, 'Please go, be kind to yourself, so that you can be kind to me willingly, not out of duty.'"

I took a deep breath. I remembered meeting my sisters as adults and hearing their pain at being abandoned by our mother. My assurance that they were spared a great deal of trauma was no comfort whatsoever to them. Their experience of being left by her was deeply scarring. From my professional experience, I understood that it was natural for parents to feel unhappy, overwhelmed or resentful sometimes, all signs that they needed support, cheerleading, comfort. I also saw that with a small amount of it from the likes of my team of social workers, and only for a short period of time, they could get back on track with themselves and each other. With that support they could rekindle their connection and make substantial changes to co-create a healthy, stable atmosphere for their children.

As I reflected on my own childhood, I felt – and still do – very strongly that it was everyone's responsibility to make sure every child in a community was fed, clothed, supported, loved, educated and integrated. I am still convinced if that sentiment is put into practice, no child will suffer. As a little girl and teenager, I had benefitted greatly from the generosity, care, support and guidance of many adults outside my family, like my German teacher, Marilyn, who provided unwavering encouragement to me and practical help. Nevertheless, I still wondered how my parents might have responded if they had received the kind of help my team had offered, and what difference it would have made to me.

Godfrey continued talking. "Duty is such a painful energy. I'm asking people to work on themselves so that they can be with others out of real willingness, also meeting needs of their own. I say, please don't do anything for anybody else until you've seen what beautiful need you are meeting for yourself. That doesn't make you selfish. It makes you real. Human beings don't do things out of duty naturally, they do things out of duty only to get into denial of responsibility."

I took my eyes off the road for a second to look at him. "Having worked in child protection for so long, Godfrey, that is hard for me to hear. I've spent a large portion of my working life training teams to help parents navigate the responsibility of being a parent. I have an issue with parents abandoning their children."

He pressed on with his point. "I would love parents who are unhappy being a parent to go away in their minds, to take an imaginary ticket to a faraway country and start reflecting on how much they love their children, love their family and how they would feel after leaving them. They might start missing their children, then feel lonely. If that imaginary experience can give them that boost of love, instead of duty, then that war has been won, and they have found a sustainable energy for healthy relationships."

Maybe this was what I had been trying to say when I spoke of commitment as a passion. "I see where you're coming from. Do you know that Zen story about offering tea to your enemy, poisoning his cup and then accidentally mixing up who gets what and drinking the toxic brew yourself? I think resentment is like that, you poison yourself."

Godfrey nodded. "Obligation is the same. I love to do what I'm doing out of a real heart energy. As I give, I am also given to; the energy I am giving will replenish itself. It means I can keep on doing what I'm doing as I care for those who are important to me."

I was curious how Godfrey's views impacted the course of his life. "How do you relate this to your experience as a father and your first divorce?"

"Oh, I have huge regrets, enormous regrets about having left my wife and my children. I thought I was just leaving an impossible relationship with my spouse. Instead, I basically lost my children. The 'other woman' I fell in love with during my marriage didn't want children around in her flat. At that time, I was in great financial straits and would have been unable to move anywhere big enough to accommodate even one child living with us.

My regret is that I wasn't able to welcome my children into my life after separating from my wife. So, to a large extent, I lost contact with them, they lost trust in me. I tried to get on with my life in other spheres, hoping that time would work things out for me and bring my children closer one day. But that didn't happen."

"When I've seen you with your children, I see healthy relationships. They are so fond of you. There's a lot of loyalty, commitment, and a lot of love coming from you too. How did you achieve that?"

"I love hearing that. But when you say commitment, that gets me back to obligation. I hear, 'You're a father and you have to do things even if you don't want to!'"

I sighed in frustration, thinking we hadn't got anywhere with our conversation at all. In a last-ditch attempt to challenge his thinking, I asked: "So, for you there is no way that commitment can be something beautiful, Godfrey?"

"If it is from the energy that says, 'I love doing this', then it doesn't require commitment or a promise on anybody's part. I just love doing it and it is meeting deep-seated aspirations in me. One couple I admire have been married for over thirty years and they renegotiate their marriage every three months. They have a special meeting, each person speaks for twenty minutes while the other listens, present, aware and attentive. And they both answer a seventy-five-point questionnaire they have developed."

"Good grief!" Twenty minutes of reflection I could imagine easily, but a long questionnaire?

"Yes, I am astounded too, they've been doing that four times a year for thirty years. When I see them now, they look as fresh as when I first met them."

"What would you say to someone who says that's just not feasible?"

"You can only know if you try it!"

Madame SatNav interrupted our conversation with a firm instruction to take the next exit. We had just arrived on the northern edge of the Rocade, the bypass that encircles Bordeaux, and I had apparently missed a turning and we were now on the ring road west of the city, instead of east. I kept straight on confident we would eventually reach the turnoff south from this direction.

Red-faced, Godfrey shouted: "Turn back!"

"Check the map; we can go this way." I handed it to him.

"Listen to Madame SatNav, we're going the wrong way!" Godfrey gesticulated wildly.

"No, I can get us through this way. We'll get there; we're just going the other way around the city centre."

"You have to turn off, we're on the wrong road!" More handwaving as Godfrey raised his voice.

"Check the map!" I insisted, pointing to where we were. "Just look at it, you'll find the ring road, I'm sure".

"It's not going to help us!" Godfrey shouted and stared out of the window, refusing to confirm our route.

Madame SatNav continued to repeat, "At the next exit turn right …. At the next exit…" I snapped the volume off.

The pair of them were getting to me.

I stabbed my finger at the map on my passenger's knee. "Just check it, will you? Jeez!"

I moved into the slow lane while I waited for his response. Nothing. He threw the map into the footwell. A wave of dislike for Godfrey and his unwillingness to help crashed through my body. Who was this person I'd agreed to drive all the way to the south of France? I pulled into the next layby, got out of the car and lit a cigarette. Smoke bellowed out of my nose. I was fuming.

Ten minutes later I had recovered my composure and gestured that we get back in the car. We drove in silence for a while until I felt calm enough to break the ice. "What just happened?"

Godfrey spoke softly, looking straight through the windscreen. "I suppose I felt quite desperate, scared. I thought, she doesn't know where we're going but the GPS knows exactly how to get us back on the road to Montolieu."

"Thing is Godfrey, I don't like turning around. I just wanted to get my bearings and keep going. I was confident we would find a shortcut."

"And, I thought, we could end up at the North Pole. I've got to stop her!" He was exaggerating for comic relief, making a peace offering. He smiled at me. The tension in the car started to evaporate.

"Godfrey, I did hear your panic. I wanted to calm you down by giving you the map. Did you notice that the road was choc-a-block in the opposite direction? I really didn't want to get stuck there."

"Ah, I didn't see that." He turned in his seat as if to see what I meant. "Wow, we could have lost another hour. I suppose I wanted to beat you up about driving on without knowing where you were." This was typical Godfrey, using violent imagery spoken with a soft voice and a smile to demonstrate the absurdity of a situation. "And then, I don't remember what happened." He laughed, feigning amnesia with a hand to his head.

"Godfrey …"

He ventured the truth. "Actually, I couldn't read the tiny font on the map."

Everything became clear to me. "You couldn't see it! What if you had just told me that? I wish I had thought to ask you!"

He confessed, "I was so unwilling to look at the map because I had no idea which part to actually look at. And when you pointed to where we were, I didn't trust you." He looked at me abashed and grinned sheepishly.

"That was exactly the message that came across, Gobby, your lack of trust! Dammit! I suppose me getting indignant didn't help much either." He giggled at my using his know-all nickname and we fell back into gentle, teasing banter, squabbling like siblings over whose fault it was we had bickered.

I let out a sigh of relief as I saw the sign for the A62 to the south. We were back on track, in more ways than one. "Know what I think, Professor Earwig?"

Godfrey snorted loudly.

I continued, "We needn't have used so many words arguing about whether to turn back or not. If you had just said, 'Lorna, I don't trust you,' I could have answered, 'Oh, just bog off!' It would have all been over a lot quicker!"

He asked quietly, "What is it that makes me trust a machine, I wonder? Although I do override the GPS if I know exactly where I am. I know it's good to have maps in the car, but it's also good to have a magnifying glass at my age!"

"Godfrey, this has been ten minutes of rehashed quarrel, is there any learning in it for us?"

"That Godfrey's a prick?" he suggested.

"You're not getting out of it that easily! My takeaway is this: When I'm overwhelmed and you are panicking, there is no point in me asking you for help. Physically, you are here in the car with me, but internally, you are lying on the floor screaming."

"And then you need to realise the little boy is having a tantrum." Godfrey's tone was sarcastic, but I took it as a request for forgiveness.

"Simply telling you why I'm driving straight on definitely wouldn't have helped, because you couldn't trust that. You need hard facts. Like a traffic sign or a map as a backup."

"Yes, if I see scientific backup for someone's word, that's good."

"Right then, I am going to get certificates made that state: 'Lorna's sense of direction has been scientifically proven to be correct'. Then, when you doubt my navigation skills in future, I can show it to you."

"I do trust that you are a good driver. I trust you." His voice was tender, reassuring.

I laughed, unbelieving.

Any stickiness between us had melted away. I rubbed my shoulder muscles, which had been tense for too long. We were now the only car on a three-lane road with no vehicle in sight, in front or in the rear-view mirror. I rested my wrists on the steering wheel, letting the car drive without a care for the road markings and we slowly drifted into a different lane.

"Why did you do that?" Godfrey sat up straight in his seat. "It's vile. Really scary! You didn't wink."

"Wink?"

"Indicate."

"Just changing lanes." I yawned. "Loads of room, look, not a thing on the road. It's like dancing on the tarmac," I teased him, slowly changing lanes again.

His words shot at me like rapid gunfire. "I trust you, except when you don't wink. I trust you, except when you accelerate. I trust you, except when you don't anticipate. I trust you, when you don't brake hard."

"What's the alternative to me braking hard? I could hit something!" I was enjoying myself.

"If you anticipate and look out for what all the other cars are doing, you don't need to brake hard. A good chauffeur never lets his passenger feel any movement in the car, acceleration is gentle, right to left is gentle."

"Well Godfrey, I still have so much to learn." My turn for sarcasm.

Godfrey checked his phone. "So how long now? It's getting late."

"About two hours. We lost time around Bordeaux."

"Can you make it there without taking a break?"

"If you don't shout at me." I put on a pouting face. "Anyway, it's you who needs the pee breaks."

"If I shout, you'll drive us into a tree?" He grinned at me.

"No, this time, I'll lean over, open your passenger door, give you a wee loving nudge and drive on."

Godfrey heaved with laughter, before he shared his reflection.

"I suppose what we have talked about today, feeling scared, needing proof, getting into knots and losing control, it's like life in general," he said. "Willingness and anticipation can save the day. We can always be anticipating what we ourselves or the other person could be feeling, thinking or needing. With that in mind Lorna, I am imagining that what you meant to say just now was, you need to enjoy having me as a passenger?"

"Let's put that on the needs list!" I exclaimed.

We drove on chattering like school kids.

"Ooh, look, the Vallée de la Garonne, this is the stretch I really like! We're coming home!"

I loved the undulations of the road, rolling through the spectacularly hilly scenery, from where you can see for miles. And the light, which sharpens the beauty of everything it illuminates. Did I just imagine being able to see the Mediterranean glisten ahead of me? I could definitely see the Pyrenees to my right. Soon, we would drive through the stone-built villages of the Cathar Region, with its ruined medieval castles, one more beautiful than the next. We opened the windows to let in the smell of summer. It was past dusk and the sun was dropping fast but I could just make out fields of shy sunflowers, rows of them spreading in every direction with their heads closed.

We passed the last hour of our journey singing into the night and ending with one of my favourite Irish ditties, Wild Mountain Thyme, almost in harmony. Both of us were looking forward to seeing everyone at the Peace Factory.

Finally, we arrived in the village square, where we were met by my friend Gundi and her husband Frank, one of the trainers, waving to us from the familiar little restaurant. We were far too late for supper. We had learned from painful past experience that the restaurant stopped serving as soon as its evening stock of food had been served.

Arriving at Montolieu for the third time really did feel like a family reunion. This year, I would stay in the trainers' accommodation, a short walk from the main venue, a former tannery that was now home to many artists, and Louise, who organised the retreat. This year I was to support the trainer team offering one-to-one empathy sessions to participants in a space outside of the workshops. I was excited.

I was also looking forward to catching up with Gundi. We always had fun together. While the trainers prepared for the participants to arrive, we would picnic and swim at some beauty spot, usually a lake near the village. The days before the training were like the run up to Christmas. We buzzed with anticipation, not knowing what kind of folk were coming. Would they be from Germany, France, the US, New Zealand, Asia, like last time? Would the attendees be packed with familiar faces like the trainer team, or would there be new friends to make? It didn't matter. We knew the experience would be rich and meaningful, full of fun and connections.

CHAPTER 10

NEEDY NEEDS

The first time Godfrey and I met as professional equals was in late 2014 at a three-day training event in Luxembourg. The first of its kind, the forum was attended by about forty other certified trainers all working internationally, most of them familiar with each other's work, writing and contributing to the development of NVC. The purpose was to exchange ideas and information about current projects and honour the spread of Nonviolent Communication globally.

Arriving by minibus from the airport at the venue, a youth hostel in Remerschen, a small wine-growing town in the south east of the country in the enchanting Moselle Valley, I took in the gentle hills lined with vineyards and interrupted by lakes. I loved it. The hostel was close to a nature reserve and thermal baths, but the agenda was so tightly knit that my bathing suit was to remain in my suitcase.

As the sessions got underway, Simon, a filmmaker, captured moments of celebration, interviews and personal video messages, which he compiled onto a DVD to send to Marshall, who was no longer actively teaching and reputed to be in ill-health, although that was not openly discussed within the community. Introductions made, we dispersed to attend 'open space' events in which anyone could offer topics for discussion or present their work or simply get to know one another. Information about what was happening at what session was posted on an information board. Casting my eyes over the array of proposed activities, a session on sharing experiences of working with NVC within organisations caught my attention. This was my bread and butter. The attendance of two staff members from the Center for Nonviolent Communication, Marshall's US-based international business, confirmed my choice. I wanted to connect with them especially to discuss collaboration with the German-speaking NVC non-profit organisation, DACH, I had co-founded.

Godfrey attended the session too. Revered as one of the elders in the group of about fifteen people, he began to recount a training he had facilitated with a project team at the European Commission.

"I was once called to assist a division where there had been a lot of upset between a male colleague, let's call him Paul, and a team of about seven women. One morning, when Paul was at another meeting, the women reported to me that, although they all held equal status within the organisational hierarchy, Paul came across as 'bossy' and they clearly didn't like this. I decided to conduct a mediation. Taking on the role of Paul, I invited his female colleagues to speak with me and tell me what they thought of me. They didn't take much encouraging; the atmosphere was charged with pent-up emotion. After a short while, they began to enjoy venting. They accused him of withholding information, of making group decisions without consulting them. They saw him as a loner and a bully."

Godfrey continued: "In the role of Paul, instead of responding by attacking them, I guessed their feelings and needs and expressed mine without judgement or frustration. I remember saying that I had a need for safety, that it was difficult for me to trust other people.

I found it hard to trust that the women were doing their jobs. The really big one was that it was hard for me to trust that I had a place in the universe and this job was my opportunity to have one, whatever the cost to other people. I witnessed a shift in the team's reactions, which moved from acrimony, arms crossed, faces bent down, eyes staring at the floor, to increased eye contact, and smiling at each other and 'Paul'. In just a few hours the women started to respond to me differently.

After lunch, the actual Paul joined to the session. The team welcomed him, which seemed to unsettle him at first as it was very different to the communication he was used to. But that welcome made him very welcoming of them and hey presto, they were into a new relationship.

I resumed my role as a training facilitator and presented some ideas on power in group dynamics and how in NVC we focus very clearly on feelings and needs in whatever we hear or speak. And that was where Paul's learning began. Until that time, he had not been aware that his needs were being met at the expense of other peoples'. He corroborated the needs I had expressed during the role-play. He remarked that he felt seen as a human being and was relieved to learn that, although his colleagues were upset, he had only been doing his best to meet his needs. The group of 'enemies' didn't see him as an enemy anymore.

By the end of the training, the people who had asked me to come were really surprised at the difference within the team; they didn't believe there could be such radical change in such a short time."

This was an experience I could relate to easily, that almost magical shift during a mediation, when two people look into each other's faces after a morning of accusations, insinuations and frustration and suddenly a light goes on behind their eyes. It still gives me goose bumps. You can almost see the moment the anger lifts from their features, replaced with surprise, curiosity and relief. If someone in a leadership role achieves this, then the whole atmosphere within the team can be transformed. My friend and colleague Andrea called this a moment of 'Herzspitzenberührung', which translates roughly as 'when the tips of the hearts briefly touch'.

Godfrey continued telling other stories. Session participants were really interested in his work at NATO, and especially in the type of language used in most companies and organisations and how different that was to the teachings of NVC. Another member of the group began to speak about a new NVC handbook she had just finished editing. I had contributed a chapter describing my experience putting NVC into practice as a CEO. I was nudged to answer some questions and after recounting a few anecdotes detailing my experience, I finished by saying that I had tried out different strategies to improve teamwork in order to meet my need for ease *at work*.

I saw Godfrey's steely eyes narrow and focus on me, before he spoke to the room: "Needs are universal, there is no need for ease at work. That is not a need. Work is a strategy."

"I would completely agree with you there."

He continued: "Then I would love to hear you speak of your need for ease and hear everything relating to work stated as observations. In that fashion we can agree among ourselves on the facts of the case. You may mention your feelings or not, but please then talk about the universal need, which is shared by your listeners, as being a need for 'ease' and not 'ease at work'."

I stared at my friend. This was to be the moment, my litmus test as an equal, Godfrey challenging me publicly with a group of other

NVC trainers watching. Unbeknown to them, we had been arguing about the unattached nature of needs for many months previously.

Godfrey pressed on. "I get very worried when I hear anyone mix up a need with a strategy, i.e. a preference for a concrete action. Any practical suggestion should not be mixed with the word 'need', like 'I need you to make my work day easier'. That puts tremendous pressure on the person who is listening, who also has a need for choice. It sounds as if there is only one option at one particular time and you are the one dictating it."

I took a deep breath. "So, when you hear me speak of my need for ease at work, are you concerned that I am not aware of that distinction between a need and strategy and you'd like me to be clear?"

"Yes. I'm worried about just one thing you implied and this is that a CEO has a need for ease at work. She doesn't. The need for ease is within the CEO as a person, simply the need for ease, like everyone else has. That need is universal."

A rigid stillness gripped the room.

Godfrey persisted: "A need for ease can be met through a thousand different strategies; it doesn't have to be at work. We inherited the concept of NVC from Marshall, and needs as a central element are not attached to any person, any one thing, or any action."

By this time, I had been an NVC trainer for more than a decade and the concept was crystal clear to me. I couldn't grasp why he was nit-picking in front of everyone as we had had this exact conversation before. My eyes fixed on Godfrey and I wondered – had I maybe been stealing the limelight?

I gave up trying to show him I was listening and switched to expressing what was in my head and heart at that moment. "I'd like to clarify something. I am totally aware of the distinction between needs and strategies and am in full agreement that it is important. I was speaking passionately about my experience and the longing underpinning my motivation to introduce NVC into my organisation. I was not teaching the concept of NVC, and we are all certified trainers here who fully understand the distinction. It was colloquial if you like, maybe 'street giraffe'."

Marshall had coined this term to describe the conversational use of empathic language.

"I'm one hundred percent in line with that. However, I still carry this big fear that comes from talk about street giraffe. That scares the living daylights out of me. I hate street giraffe when it compromises the concept of needs."

"Your concern is about the integrity of NVC?"

Godfrey nodded vigorously. The icy atmosphere in the room began to thaw. Some feet shuffled, faces relaxed and a few folks reached for their cups of coffee and biscuits.

Godfrey, it seemed, wanted to have an academic discussion around the compatibility of the core concept of NVC and everyday language. I was all up for it and forgot the eyes on us. I slipped back into our cosy driving chatter.

"Well, this might upset you, Godfrey, but I'm going to risk it. I would like to propose that NVC is not so much about words, but about creating connection. Using the language of feelings and needs is a kind of practice tool. Albeit very useful, it's simply a way to train the mind and liberate it from structured thoughts in order to get our real message across. If it is not facilitating an honest, empathic connection, then it can seem mechanical. If I am speaking my truth, what is alive inside me right now, then I am conveying my reality. When I mentioned my needs as a CEO being a need for ease at work, you could have tuned into my experience of exhaustion, my deep desire to co-create an enjoyable work atmosphere, instead of correcting me. Words are not reality. What's real are the underlying desires being conveyed."

I noticed Godfrey holding his breath, still listening, totally focussed.

"C'mon then, tell me what is it that annoyed you about what I just said."

"I get upset when I fear the core of NVC is being changed, weakened. We inherited from Marshall a really beautiful mindset which Robert [a trainer from the US] evolved into the concepts of 'needy needs', 'classical NVC needs' and then 'Aha needs'."

We were getting into the detail. I glanced around the room. It would be the first time some of the folk present were exposed to these concepts. "Marshall didn't make that distinction," I countered.

Marshall stuck to language that described hidden demands behind needs and encouraged people to take responsibility for meeting their needs by detaching themselves from just one solution, for instance, a person with a need for comfort insisting that a specific person be the chosen one to meet that need by giving them a hug. Robert's concept of the 'Aha moment' goes further, describing when a person can identify the deep, hidden longing behind an emotion. It is usually accompanied by a sigh of self-recognition. I wasn't convinced that Robert's descriptions of needs were helpful really, but I kept my mouth shut.

Needy Needs

Godfrey replied: "I love that distinction! I would love to bring people the easiest possible access to 'Aha needs'."

"If I want to fully understand someone who speaks, thinks and behaves very differently from me, it can be really helpful to use colloquial language to make my intention for connection more comprehensible. Street giraffe, everyday language, is not necessarily a bad thing, it can actually help create the 'Aha moment'."

Gotcha there, I thought with confidence. I noticed people writing notes, others seemed riveted, two had settled on some cushions on the floor and had closed their eyes.

Godfrey slumped a little and sighed. "I don't say it's a bad thing. I say it's awash with danger, the danger of diluting what a need really is. My passion is to see human beings connecting more. And if needs get diluted with strategies, I'm convinced that's not going to happen."

I wondered why he could not see my point. "Godfrey, I believe the dilemma is this: for people who have gone through the usual education system, and then start learning the language of NVC, it is hard for them to talk naturally. If they change the way they speak too much, they stand out, sound odd and tongue-twisted when they talk about needs and feelings. NVC language can sound like a standardised formula, which creates estrangement rather than empathic connection. On the other hand, it is absolutely possible to listen or express yourself from the heart and have a snappy quick chat without losing the core of NVC."

Before he could interrupt, I seized the initiative.

"When I was working with young street kids, one young man, about fifteen years old and known as the Chief, threatened another gang member for making a decision without asking him. If I had asked him, 'Are you frustrated because your need for autonomy is not being met?' I would have lost him, it would have been easy for him to continue getting upset, dismissing me as another stupid teacher. It was much more helpful to ask, 'Are you really pissed off because you want to make your own decisions, you want a say in what happens in your life?' That was a game changer actually."

"I love that because it is a perfect way of saying the need for autonomy without mentioning the word need."

"That to me is street giraffe!" I said, feeling I had finally got my message across.

"That's fine! But street giraffe is not being taught in the way you have used it. I see the core of NVC being adulterated. I hear street giraffe is just about saying anything and then calling it a need."

"Something like 'I need you to do this at work for me' and because they've used the word need, they believe it is Nonviolent Communication?"

"Almost... Yes."

"If I had said, 'As a CEO I was really desperate for new ways to make life more fun' and not mentioned needs, you wouldn't have corrected me?" He nodded. "Do you have an expectation that trainers always and everywhere conduct their conversations in NVC?"

"I would love them to not 'conduct' their conversations in anything. I would love them to be aware, step-by-step as they are speaking, of the need they are serving."

"What about wit and banter?"

Needy Needs

"Then we are in touch with our universal need for fun!"

We both took a deep breath, smiling at each other.

"I remember our colleague Miki saying that the only way to get NVC wrong was to think there's a right way to do it." I grinned at Godfrey. "Would you say you are a something of a purist when it comes to NVC?"

"Yes, yes! I am as pure as I can be!" Laughter around the room. "And sometimes I fall well below my own standards." Godfrey paused for a moment, before he looked across at me. "I regret that I got riled. I'm still not totally sure how to combine needs consciousness and language with easy relations."

I thought about our conversations in the car. "I have often heard you remark, 'but that's not the right word' and sometimes 'I am very scared of words'. What is that about exactly?"

"I fear the words I use today will create the world I live in tomorrow. You do know that after the bomb was dropped on Hiroshima, the Americans threatened to strike at a second Japanese city if they didn't receive an unconditional surrender. The Japanese sent a carefully-worded telegram detailing the conditions under which they would surrender. There was a subtle double entendre in the Japanese message that the translator didn't recognise and misinterpreted as 'we do not surrender'. So, the Americans bombed Nagasaki. I see mini-Nagasakis of misunderstanding occurring every day. I say in every training course I give, that every time one person opens their mouth, another person misunderstands."

"We don't even have to open our mouths for that to happen."

The room rippled with chuckles. Only then, I noticed that Simon had joined the space and his camera had been rolling, I had no idea for how long. I gulped, trying to remember whether I had said anything I wished I hadn't.

One of the organising team, a petite French lady threw her arms in the air with a big smile and exclaimed, "It's time for a street giraffe lunch – let's continue at 3.00pm!"

In the canteen, Godfrey joined me in the queue and suggested we take a walk to the lake. Armed with a chunky baguette, a large piece of delicious-looking plum quetschentaart and two forks, we set off briskly through the chilled autumn air.

"Someone just asked me if I was getting back together with my ex-wife."

"Don't tell me she's here? You didn't say!" Although I had heard a lot about her, I had never met Godfrey's ex-wife and was curious and a little annoyed he hadn't pointed her out to me earlier.

"When I went around the group this morning with the microphone, I apparently rested my arm on her knee while holding up the mic for her. But I felt nothing, she was just another participant."

"Oh, good Lord! Are you OK with that?"

"I had switched into trainer mode. Especially after our conversations about trainer ethics and how I create contact between me as a trainer and the participants."

During the retreat at Montolieu, our friendship was tested. As agreed, we had met for thirty minutes everyday day as part of Godfrey's self-care programme. I had been willing to support him, but it wasn't easy and triggered childhood memories of being the caretaker of my parent's emotional stability. It was exhausting.

Needy Needs

One particular issue arose that weighed heavily on me: Godfrey's relationship with a female participant set my alarm bells ringing. She had clearly taken a shine to him. Later, he said he hadn't noticed her interest, but his behaviour, such as letting her walk arm in arm with him into the sessions, allowing intimate seating positions in the garden after workshops, giggling together in a leaning-in posture, and letting her shower in his room before supper, to me, signalled his consent. I had been concerned. And I wasn't the only one who had noticed. Even some participants were aware. My personal conviction was and is that healthy boundaries at retreats contribute to everyone feeling comfortable and as trainers our job is to facilitate learning in a way that is as safe and easy as possible.

As the #MeToo movement gathered steam and stirred a global discussion of sexual harassment, I was aware of differing opinions in the world of NVC around ethical trainer behaviour, the suggestion of guidelines and the inference of 'policing' at retreats to prevent sexual relations between trainers and participants.

At Montolieu, thinking about Godfrey and the participant, I hadn't known what to do. I had noticed Godfrey relaxing around female attention and that was pleasing to observe; he had just had a rough, lonely couple of years. I wanted him to feel loved and admired. I also recognised that empathic listening can easily be confused with sexual intimacy. Should I keep quiet and trust that Godfrey and the participant were consenting adults; after all many people met their partners at work? Should I tell someone and who would that be? Or should I confront Godfrey, challenge his intentions and risk his annoyance?

I opted for the latter.

To my surprise, Godfrey was happy to hear my feedback. He had not been aware of the small signals he was giving that he was open to a relationship, and felt glad I'd prompted him to check his intentions and his need for attention and intimacy. We arrived at a slogan to remind him.

Walking now toward the lake in Remerschen, Godfrey turned and repeated it back to me: "Keep your pants on until after the training."

I nodded.

The November sun sparkled on the water and our footsteps disturbed some ducks that flew up and overhead. I decided to change the subject.

"What do you think of our discussion back there? With everyone around us. I actually forgot they were there. But you were picking on me a bit!"

"No! I relaxed when I heard you agree that a need is universal, neither good nor bad, that it's not attached to an object, action or person. I'm happy with that. But you would have preferred some 'connection before correction'. Something like that?"

I took his arm. "Indeed. I was describing my situation at work. You could have cut me some slack. It's hard work for me having to translate the whole time from German in my head to English."

He looked at me simultaneously surprised and embarrassed as we sat on a bench in a sunny spot with a view of the water and unwrapped our baguettes.

Before I bit into mine, I said: "I really value something about that session. We got to the nitty gritty of what is the core of NVC for you and I really do share that. I just want to leave the stagnancy

I hear in NVC language. I like the idea of visiting the other person on their planet, just getting a whiff of the air they are breathing, and if I'm able to do that, it doesn't matter if I speak gobbledygook, pure needs-based language or street giraffe."

Godfrey held his fork upward as he replied, animated, "I'm very happy with the notion that it's less a matter of the words being important, but rather the underlying intention. If there is connection and the citing of the need is the vehicle to achieve that, then that's fine."

We seemed to be inching toward agreement.

"Absolutely, Godfrey. When I hear someone talking about the desire for a particular strategy, I am inspired to look behind that and stay with whatever it is they are longing for. I would then look into the detail of the desire, and explore how that can be met within the relationship. In contrast, I think that when you hear the person say they need a particular action, you see them as stuck in attachment."

"If someone comes to me with a problem like not receiving enough hugs from their partner, then I will guess at their feelings and needs and choose to work on the most important need, for example, the need for affection. I would then invite them to look at the areas of their life in which this need gets met, not just by their husband." He paused. "I've been doing that for years, but I notice that they say, 'yes, that's all very fine, but, Godfrey, what do I do now about my partner?'"

We both laughed.

"Godfrey, are you actually calling your ideas into question, now, when I have no audience or cameras rolling?"

"Maybe. I notice that some people are unhappy with my training and resist. In this example, I would typically suggest that the wife take responsibility for meeting the needs that a husband's hug would fulfil, which automatically takes the pressure off her husband and he is likely to expand, and notice the wife's needs and want to contribute to meeting them." He looked at me over his glasses. "Except, it doesn't seem to work."

"When you put your sole focus on the holy grail of an unattached need, perhaps sometimes the coach leads the client away from the problem and doesn't enable the client to activate sufficient resources to deal with it."

Godfrey pondered. "I'm discovering I want to keep pace more with the client, and only lead once they show me that they want me to. In order for that to happen, I like to generate much greater enthusiasm to listen to the details of their stories so that trust builds and they sense I am truly and deeply interested in them and not wishing to push them anywhere."

I was surprised. "What makes you think that you haven't been doing this before?"

"To a certain extent I probably have been, but I have received feedback in training groups that I seem not to care about the outcome of the issue that the client brought to the table. They are glad of the sense of personal responsibility for meeting their own needs, but are still hungry for someone to work on their very real problem. They feel abandoned."

"Then, could you shift focus to the strategy that would suit them and their problem? For instance, role-play and you take on the role of the husband, like you did with Paul and the team, or even get them to swap roles, as you did with your grandmother, and have the client ask him for a hug?"

"That's it!" Godfrey's exclamation triggered a surge of pride in me, joy that I was able to give him a helpful hint, that he was willing to ask for and accept.

We returned to the venue just in time for the afternoon sessions, waving to each other as we split off into separate groups.

The next day, Godfrey accompanied me on the minibus ride back to the airport, just to 'chum me', as my friend Aileen would say. I had been busy typing up the transcripts of our conversations so far and had given them to him to read. I was dying to know if he thought we had enough to write a book.

Godfrey replied, "Some things were moving, heart-warming and some parts of it were embarrassing. It was like when I first heard my voice as an interpreter and I thought 'who's that idiot?'"

"Let's have a good long chat about it when I help you move to Saint-Étienne next month, how's that?"

"Definitely."

At the airport Godfrey said he'd wait with me until my flight boarded. We sat down for a cup of tea.

"Did I ever tell you my story about the shepherd?"

I shook my head.

"My second wife and I were in Turkey on a riding holiday with a group of about twelve people. It was so thrilling because we were sleeping rough under bivouacs in a field each night." I shivered. Camping was not my idea of a relaxing break. "One morning, as the sun rose, we woke up to the sound of our Turkish guide, who only spoke two words of French, 'moi' and 'fort', screaming at a shepherd who, terrified, was holding a twelve-bore shotgun to his head. My first thought was, 'that gun might actually go off by accident; I'm going to intervene.' Now I really didn't want to see myself in a Turkish prison, but I moved towards them and gently inserted my hands between the two men and moved them apart, all the while speaking to the shepherd quietly in English. I was quite sure he didn't understand a word, but I said something like: 'Are you alarmed when you see these foreigners camping on the land that has been entrusted to you, without your permission, and you're upset because this is your field?' Then, he lowered the gun slowly, stretched out his hand, shook mine and gave me the broadest smile that I had ever witnessed."

"Wow." I sat open-mouthed.

I also reflected that he'd just confirmed that it's not really the words that matter so much as the intention and nonverbal signs we send when we want to achieve peaceful connection.

"I realised later that the reason the guide hadn't pushed me away was because I was the oldest in the group, the 'unassailable elder', and he didn't want a problem with me in addition to the shepherd. I didn't care if I died, but I cared deeply for the people we were travelling with. After the event, it wasn't the fear that stayed with me. It moved me to a realisation of how precious life is. And the relief at the outcome." Tears started welling up in his eyes. "Lord knows what might have happened if I hadn't got up. At the end of a gun, life just stops."

"Depending on which end of the gun you're at!"

"It doesn't matter. It could have ended the guide's life, the shepherd's or mine. Both ends of the gun are simply wrong; there isn't a right end to be on. It's a gun."

Needy Needs

I noticed two older ladies smiling fondly at us, probably assuming we were father and daughter saying farewell at the airport.

We hugged each other as I grabbed my hand luggage, detecting there had been a change in the quality of the time we spent together. I still loved listening to Godfrey's stories and us poking fun at each other, but our relationship had evolved, and we were making adjustments to accommodate those changes without any conscious decisions. It was like I had grown and we were meeting on a more even playing field. I sensed that Godfrey perceived it too.

CHAPTER 11

F'R'AMILY

As it turned out, Godfrey completed the move from Brussels to Saint-Étienne without my help. Instead, we planned for me to visit and for us to take a week out of our busy schedules to focus on the book. Godfrey also wanted to introduce me to his new partner, Geneviève, who lived nearby, when she returned from a short trip. He had relocated to the small town southwest of Lyon to be as close to her as possible. He really wanted to make an effort with this relationship.

Godfrey met me at the train station. As we walked to his flat in the town centre, he told me that Saint-Étienne had once been a hub for arms production, as well as the manufacture of ribbons. I pulled my suitcase along the uneven pavement, passing boarded-up shop windows, navigating overflowing dustbins and workmen's vans loading office equipment. Signs of an economic slump were obvious. I was relieved to arrive at his new home. As he opened his front door we were confronted with unpacked boxes and piles of books and bags. My heart sank at the chaos. It was clear he had yet to really settle in. I thought about the week we'd spent a year ago packing all his things and recognised some of the same possessions scattered about the room.

Godfrey put the kettle on. I found a spot to sit. We were catching up on each other's news and mutual friends, when Godfrey's phone rang. His face lit up as he began to Facetime in French with his sixteen-year-old granddaughter Juliette. As he spoke, his features softened and his voice dipped. He seemed choked and his eyes filled with tears, which he brushed away with his fingertips. When they'd finished talking, Godfrey blew his nose loudly, and turned to me. "Right, where were we?"

"I'm not going to ignore your tears this time dear, what touched you so?" I asked.

"I'm moved at her emotional response. She was excited to be in Canada and now she is eager to be back. She's just cleared customs. I was the first person she had called. She's had quite a horrific experience arriving in Brussels because she left her passport on the plane and couldn't enter Belgium and had to wait with the police. I can imagine her, at sixteen, feeling quite distressed. I kind of took it on, imagining her feelings and that must have brought me to tears."

I sipped my tea. "You do cry easily. What do you think goes on for you when someone is moved?"

Godfrey sat back on the chair. "No one's ever asked that question before. I thought it was normal with someone close to me to be sensitive to any emotions that are going on in them."

"Maybe. Are you also remembering being scared travelling, losing your passport and needing help?" I thought about how often Godfrey searched for important items he thought he'd lost but had just mislaid, his keys, phone, wallet.

"Yes, but that's sympathy though, not empathy."

It was an important distinction to make. Marshall spoke of this difference long before neurobiological research showed how each register differently in the brain. Working with the Samaritans for many years listening to suicidal callers at the other end of the phone line desperate for help, I developed a metaphor to help the team understand empathy: we each live in our own house, we can visit other people's, feel into their experience, but we don't move in and take on their emotions. That doesn't help anyone. When we feel sympathy, we might feel pity or sorrow for someone's misfortune, but our attention is on our own experience, rather than being attentive and present with the other person, guessing their feelings and needs. When our focus shifts to them, that is empathy.

I asked Godfrey, "When you hear how moved she is, then you are moved too, the mirror neurons firing in your brain?"

He nodded. His lower lip trembled. "Even if I am simultaneously getting in touch with that part of me that still needs some recognition of tough times I've been through, how my need for comfort and safety has not always been met, I keep it to myself while I'm listening to her, because that's my story, not hers."

I wondered if there was more to his reaction. "Watching you listen to her fright at the airport, I wonder, were you moved because she was sharing it with you first, which also met your need to matter? Like a reminder of your connection?"

"Yes," Godfrey wiped a tear from his cheek. "As I am a 'non-father' and a 'non-grandfather', any moment when I am being treated as a grandfather is moving."

"What do you mean? You are a father and a grandfather. And I bet you were a good dad when you were with your children."

"I was a very good father to very small children. As soon as they started to speak, I wasn't that interested."

"Now that surprises me, because language is your thing! That could sound a bit mean."

"There's something very tender about a parent's relationship with a baby in the middle of the night. I don't think any of my children woke up at night without me participating in their care. And I know that was unusual at the time. I hear such different stories from family and friends, like the man goes on snoring and the woman gets out of bed when the child needs changing, feeding. But I did all those things, every time."

"Because you're such a light sleeper do you think?"

"No, because I love fairness. I also took them for walks, to the park and all that. And when I left Rolande, it was really difficult for me. I didn't realise I was also leaving my children. In fact, now I recognise that I actually abandoned them. Most men have some kind of custodianship of the children. I didn't fight for that. They were with their mother every day of the year. Sometimes we met for a meal. And I do remember a week-long holiday in Switzerland when all of us were together."

"Do you think they resented not having you around?"

"Yes, I think so. Yes. My daughter threatened to write a book. If she does, I'll have to have her sent to gaol or something." He chuckled. "I was interested and engaged with them when they were old enough to hold conversations about the important things in life, when they were adolescents. Now, I think they have given up on me in a way. I'm too distant. They rarely call me, and I just forget to call them."

I looked at Godfrey, feeling that he was being a little hard on himself. I reminded him of the connectedness I had witnessed between him and his daughter in Brussels and Virginia's family in England.

He nodded. "There seem to be no hard feelings though, they seem to have accepted that I'm just like that. Which is a bit sad really. I hope that to some degree I will prove to the world that I can change. I'm not sure though."

"You could invite them all for Christmas, to meet Geneviève?"

Godfrey threw back his head and hooted. "We don't have room for one hundred and fifty people! I've got thirteen grandchildren. When we do meet up, there's always great excitement and they want me to stay with them. It is lovely. I remember what a gentle Irish mother once said when I asked, 'Who is your favourite child?' She replied, 'The one I'm with!' That's the case for me too."

"They are all connected by their love for you. I have seen that between you."

Godfrey put his hands together as if in prayer and thanks. Another involuntary tear rolled down his cheek.

Walking back from lunch at his favourite bistro, we waited at the edge of the tram tracks until the lights indicated it was safe to cross. I was in a rather dreamy state, still savouring the chocolate, raspberry and caramel dessert I'd consumed, and feeling the effect of the digestif. We watched a young mother fasten her two children into the backseat of an SUV parked on the other side of the road. As she climbed back into the driver's seat, her young son jumped out of the vehicle onto the pavement. She got out, put him back inside, slammed the door and got back in. He jumped out again. She ran round to the open passenger door, slapped him hard and stuffed him back inside the car. We could hear her shouting as she pointed her finger at him.

I stood there, gobsmacked, as the car accelerated down the road. Godfrey slipped his arm through mine and we walked on in silence. Back at his apartment, slumped in a comfy armchair, surrounded by piles of books, I was still thinking about the scene we had witnessed.

"I'm shocked at myself for not doing anything," I said, and sighed. "Watching domestic violence, silenced by loyalty, was such a big part of my childhood. I wish I had reacted differently to that mother in the town centre just now."

Godfrey suggested making some tea.

Handing me a mug, he said, "I love a story that Marshall told about when he was in a supermarket and saw a woman with a small child sitting in the shopping trolley. The child kept reaching left and right grabbing things from the shelves. The mother got increasingly frustrated and eventually slapped the child, who then started screaming his head off. Marshall turned to the mother and gave her empathy without condemning the child. Then he saw the look of relief on the child's face.

By supporting the mother, he was supporting the child by trying to make the world such a friendly place for the parent that they didn't need to be angry at the child any more. I would love to live in that world, where if we see stress between two people, we carry both of them in our hearts, and not support one side against the other, which mostly happens when we involve ourselves in other people's disputes. In the cases of abused children, I would like to see us, as neighbours, friends and witnesses not reporting the parents to the police, but instead feeling comfortable with just giving the necessary support to the parents in order that they do not harm the child. That, to me, would be a different world."

I nodded slowly. "Godfrey, that does happen. It's just not so easy to do, even for me, and I have twenty-five years of practice! When I worked in child protection outreach – and this was post-Reunification when money was flowing from the German state and social workers were involved in developing new rules and practices – even then, we often dealt with cases where a child was being abused and we wanted to work with the parents, but the state would only finance counselling if the child was 'worked with'."

Godfrey raised a questioning eyebrow.

I explained. "Meaning the social worker's time spent with the child was paid for, time with the parents was not. It was a dilemma we tried to resolve with careful reporting, so the state could see we were working with the child, but in fact our focus was mainly on the parents. As for the children, they got support if they needed it. Most were understandably wary of being seen as 'the problem' by becoming the focus of the solution. They were simply relieved that the abuse and violence had stopped. And our workplan confirmed the children's perception that it was their parents' behaviour that needed correction, not theirs. It was astounding how impactful our work was, counselling without judgement and training parents in empathic skills. It meant they could use alternative strategies to find peace and quiet for example, or rest or respect, other than hitting their children." I paused. "I wish I'd intervened just now."

Godfrey switched into trainer mode. "Let's take a look at that situation, the needs being met or unmet. I think the child's behaviour, getting out of the car, was failing to meet the mother's need for movement. She wanted to go. After several attempts, she was obviously totally frustrated and overwhelmed."

"Maybe she was also worried for his safety because of the traffic. He was probably in a lot of pain, though. Being hit, especially in public, strips away so much dignity."

"He could have had an unmet need for autonomy."

"I also recognised his need for fun; he thought it was hilarious that she got out the car, put him in, then he got out again, and so on."

"After she slapped him, she probably had an unmet need for harmony, peace and to contribute to another's wellbeing."

"She was definitely not experiencing inner peace as she drove away. More likely she was tense, heart racing, all sorts of physical sensations going on."

We paused.

Godfrey began. "If only she had been able to take a deep breath and think, 'Wow, I've just slapped a human being!' Then reflect about what need of hers was not met by her slap. It could be gentleness, or consideration, connection, respect. Basic human dignity. My belief is that if a parent can do that, take a pause, then a lot of the pain starts to settle. There is space to see the needs they met by inflicting the punishment, their unmet needs afterwards, and the needs the victim was trying to fulfil in doing whatever they were doing. That would be a big step towards the world I want to live in, which is a world where everybody will listen and be heard."

It reminded me of a case I worked on twenty years before. "There was a father who sexually abused his eight-year-old stepdaughter. I remember him talking with me in a counselling session, for the first time ever, about being raped himself as an eight-year-old, by his father.

He said he didn't know how to express his love for his daughter in any other way, simultaneously confusing love with sexual behaviour. I found him truly credible; he had never really understood his own pain or been heard as a victim. He said that seeing the anguish in his stepdaughter's face helped him in some way feel understood for his own experience." I paused. "But, for me, first and foremost, we must make sure that whoever has experienced violence finds safety, in this case a child within its family. That comes before anything else. And what you say falls short of this aspect."

"I do know that by listening to somebody who has a real problem with his or her own violent behaviour, it is not guaranteed that the person will stop."

I put down my mug. We appeared to have arrived back at a familiar place; a discussion about the limits of empathy. This time I asked him a critical question. "Is it a shortcoming of NVC that when we show empathy to people who have behaved badly that it is not guaranteed that they will change?"

"No, it is a shortcoming in human beings who have expectations of this thing called NVC. I don't want empathy to be seen as a solution, rather as an art of living."

"So, you're saying empathic parenting is like an art and a good parent is someone whose needs are met?" I wanted to pin Godfrey down on this point and move on.

"I don't think anyone can be a parent to a child, help a child blossom, if there are too many major needs not being met. It's difficult for someone who has been, or is, too unhappy in their lives, to keep an open mind towards the needs of their children. It's almost as if violence is a twisted substitute for empathic connection, a call for it."

This interpretation of violence jarred with me, but I agreed that any sign of it sounded an alarm bell, was a call for change.

"I remember you saying nobody needs parents. Do you still believe that?"

"Absolutely, I believe it really deeply. Nobody needs parents and nobody needs children. When you say a parent is an unworthy parent, that parent should not necessarily be deprived of their parenting rights. In an ideal world, you'd see what needs a child has regarding parenting – a need for tenderness, affection, structure, support, ease – and if a parent can't provide them, someone else can. Hence, the protective adoption of children. I think many children who have been adopted may agree that to stay with their natural parents would have been a disaster in their lives."

I thought of my younger sister, whom I had only met as an adult a few years before. She had been adopted at birth by a wealthy family and was still angry at our mother for giving her and her twin brother away, particularly as I, although two years old and in foster care when they were born, had ultimately remained with our birth parents. From my point of view, she definitely got the better end of the deal having been spared the poverty, domestic violence and emotionally unstable environment I endured as a child. I would have loved someone to have intervened and removed me from my unreliable parents' care. But before I opened my mouth to tell Godfrey, I felt a wash of gratitude for my friends, the chosen family I had created for myself and that came tumbling out first.

"I'm so appreciative of my 'framily', friends in my heart with whom the connection remains no matter what. We're bound, bonded, 'verbunden', as we say in German, there is a passion to keep that fire burning," I said.

"I love your idea of 'framily'. Lorna the more I think about it, the more I sense it just being a good word for love. Instead of commitment and the idea of duty and obligation – that would be the killer word for me."

I didn't want to discuss commitment again. "I think a lot of people in NVC circles use the idea of duty to wriggle out of agreements, let people down, change their minds."

Godfrey thought for a second. "Marshall also said, 'If you meet a need of yours and some need of any one of the other seven or eight billion people in the world is not met through your decision, then you may get what you need, but with a sour taste in your mouth." I handed him a corkscrew and pointed to a bottle of Pinot Noir on the table before I answered.

"I am in a dilemma with this. Haven't we talked about this a lot already?" I sounded hesitant, not wishing to open up another conversation about obligation, but also sensing this topic was still a complex one for him. "If I want something to happen really badly and, for example, you don't want it to, but say yes anyway, I don't want to blame or shame you if you change an agreement, but I do want to be seen. I want to know that I matter and am cared for, whether I can rely on you." I paused. "Just thinking about my early years, it was hard for me as a child to experience my parents not doing what they said they would do. I learned very early that adults were not reliable. In a relationship I need to know I can depend on you. I know trust is not something you can get; it can only be given. For me, you helping me to trust you, living a caring connection, that's 'framily'."

I smiled shyly. This was probably the closest I had ever come to a declaration of platonic love for Godfrey.

We had a week of work ahead of us before our respective partners joined us. I was excited for Godfrey to meet Ivan. He was one of my very first boyfriends and, thirty years later, we had rekindled our romance around the same time Godfrey had fallen in love with Geneviève. I knew Godfrey would love Ivan, who was already keen to meet him having heard so much about him, and I was excited to meet the woman who had settled Godfrey's roaming heart.

Later that evening, over dinner, Godfrey said: "You know, I actually hate the idea of being seen as a man relating to a woman. As you've heard me say many a time, 'I am a man like any other woman'. I'd rather think of an intimate relationship as a connection between two human beings, rather than between a male and a female. I know people who live with partners of the same sex and they have the same problems as we all do."

"We've come to know each other quite well by now Godfrey, and have followed each other's relationships. Scary question: do you think this will be your last? I do hope you stay together as long as possible." I remembered Godfrey's sadness and loneliness when he was single.

Godfrey chuckled. "Geneviève and I are going to stay together until I die, which is when I am one hundred and fifteen years of age – another thirty-five years to go. I am eighty and enjoying life a great deal."

I sipped my wine. "What is it, do you think, that keeps people in relationships, even after they've felt so much pain in their previous ones?"

We had spent hours of our friendship reflecting, analysing and empathising with each other over the challenges, sad discoveries and emotional hurdles we faced in relationships. We shared a need for freedom and autonomy, and we both had a tendency to get bored with routine.

Godfrey was quick to answer. "It's a lot to do with surprise – not being able to anticipate what comes next, like living in a house that isn't square, you never quite know where you are. In a relationship, it's the same. Focussing on needs helps relationships to be much freer. Instead of scrutinising things we do or don't do, looking at needs means we can get out of the demand energy, which seems to rear its ugly head whenever we experience intimacy and closeness. The other thing I love about relationships is that you get to talk to each other very openly. I'd never want to be without that."

Instead of working solely on the book as planned, the week passed in a blur of visits to the DIY store to buy shelving, unpacking boxes, filling the built-in cupboards of the hallway with camping gear, winter coats, tools and household devices, untangling a beautiful mobile for the living room, and hanging up pictures that I recognised from the last move.

Then, Godfrey lost some of his eyesight. We were in his kitchen chatting about the first draft of the first two chapters when he suddenly exclaimed. "I can't see the middle of the lines!"

After a call to his son Sebastian, the medical director of a hospital in Brussels, we got into a taxi and rushed to the local university hospital. Godfrey spent three days there for further tests. I remained at his flat, liaising with his son, his doctor and the medical staff, visiting him daily, bringing food and other bits he needed. Geneviève was out of town, not due back until the weekend, and I wanted to be on hand in case he was discharged. I knew I was good in an emergency.

Ivan postponed his trip. Alone in an unfamiliar place, I spent a lot of time wandering around the town. Although it appeared that Godfrey's eyesight impairment was a temporary condition, his illness stirred some macabre thoughts in my head. I had seen him really scared. His jokes about living for another thirty-five years were clearly just that. And the task of recording our friendship became more urgent. Godfrey really was 'fRamily' to me.

CHAPTER 12

A WHIRLWIND ADVENTURE

We didn't know it, but while Godfrey and I immersed ourselves in a workshop based on the mind-body connection work of American philosopher Eugene Gendlin, Hurricane Niklas was storming its way across Europe. The two-day programme held just outside Frankfurt in the spring of 2015, was led by a well-known American trainer, who had worked with Marshall since the late seventies. It was a simple and small event and actually more enjoyable than I had expected. I was surprised I knew all the other fifteen participants, who were mostly longstanding members of the German-speaking trainer community of which I was a part. Godfrey was well-known to most and was welcomed heartily.

Returning to Frankfurt by train on our way to Berlin – where we planned to spend a week at my home working on our book project and making plans to offer trainings as a team in French, English and German – Godfrey reflected on what he had learned at the workshop about procrastination, not keeping appointments, having too many projects to work on and his experience of getting distressed about it.

"I have realised that when I get distracted from something that I've undertaken to do and then don't do, I could remind myself of how much I really want to contribute to the well-being of the people involved. It really helps me to receive reminders too, like when you send me an email or text. I do hear your despair then, which echoes my own feelings, and that actually helps me to get moving."

"OK." I wondered where he was heading with this. Behind the scenes, I had been struggling for quite a while with our plans. I was really excited about his suggestions to work together, create a website and training materials, etc., but then observed myself waiting for documents, decisions and information from him. I braced myself, listening.

"And my second insight is that when I become distracted, I'm actually getting depressed. I haven't wanted to admit that to myself, because then I feel hopeless and helpless. I see myself grovelling on the floor and I can't get up." The setting sun glowed on his face as fields rushed by outside. "I'm sensing how moved I am just saying that. I immediately tell myself, 'Oh, come on Godfrey, grow up, what's all this nonsense about?' To sense that somebody is beside me in a moment like that is a great help. When I'm on the ground, I'd love someone to say, 'You're doing fine Godfrey, another couple of pulls and you'll be standing up again'."

I looked at my friend, who just months before I'd witnessed struggling with his health. "I didn't realise you were in despair when you didn't respond or do a task. I just thought you had forgotten me and the things we had planned. It's hard for me because I don't wish to pressure you. I just want to get on with my to-do list. And I lack the confidence sometimes to realise it's not a sign you've changed your mind about our projects."

"When I'm distracted or depressed, I am removed from going ahead with a project, like our book or the trainings."

"What's the solution?"

"First and foremost, I could just realise that it's happening. Then look for that little bit of support that makes it easier for me to lift my head, instead of remaining metaphorically with my face in the mud, finding it impossible to breathe."

"Goodness, what would you like me to do if you are procrastinating?"

By this time, our book project was inching forward. I had begun to write up our conversations and ask Godfrey follow-up questions to fill in the gaps. It was time-consuming and detailed work. At the same time, we were creating a portfolio of trainings that reflected our experience with multilingual teams. There was a lot to do.

"If you were able to say to me, 'I see, Godfrey, that you're into distraction and having difficulties,' that would actually be enough to get me taking the next step and lift my head."

"Naming it, in order to tame it, so to speak?"

"Exactly! It's not just up to you though, I am working on the origins of this tendency of mine to just run away when the pressure is on me." He looked out of the train window. "Having impaired eyesight worried me and I was so glad you were there. You said something about the eyes reacting to what we don't want to look at. And that got me thinking. And researching. I went to see a specialist. She asked me whether I had moved house very often. I answered that I had moved house so often that I could hardly keep track! We chatted and she concluded that circulation was an issue for me and asked if anyone in my family had had vein or artery related problems. I told her my father died of peripheral vascular disease and my grandfather had something similar too. She called this the 'Stade Circulatoire', which relates to the period of development between the end of gestation and early infancy." He paused. "It explains a lot of things."

"How so?" I was curious to hear about this specialist and what she had to say about Godfrey's restlessness.

"She described NVC and war as being facets of the same energy. That was fascinating. I told her how much war there had been in my life and how anxious my mother had been when she was pregnant with me, with bombs raining down on London and my father being away. She didn't know if he would return alive. The doctor said, 'The important thing for a soldier is to keep on the move.' And as a child rushes through life, keeping on the move to protect themselves in order not to die, the mission becomes more and more important and the moving more and more compelling. When I look at my life, I recognise some meaning in that. I live my life in a hurry, as if I have a mission to achieve."

I could think of several occasions when Godfrey had rushed on ahead, not stopping, as I raced to catch up with him. "And?"

"Well, she suggested taking her magic potions."

I raised my eyebrow. He grinned at me.

"Aurum metallicum was one. I will probably notice something happening in six to eight weeks. I don't want to be like a bunch of my other NATO colleagues who retire and die within a year, but I would love to have less of a compulsion to move and less fear that I'd die if I stopped. Since I returned from England to Belgium, I've lived in Brussels, and now Saint-Étienne and I'm still travelling across Europe teaching. Will I want to stay in my new home? I doubt it very much. If the medication works, then maybe I'll just be able to sit on a balcony in a deckchair, but that's not what I'm used to. If I don't slow down, I think I'm going to become even more disconnected."

Disembarking from the train at Frankfurt station, we met with chaos. Several special announcements regarding Niklas boomed over the concourse. Station attendants in red and blue uniforms tried to answer desperate queries from hundreds of stranded passengers. All train lines were closed. The information point was crowded with people and their suitcases, all in need of a bed for the night.

I was aware that this could be daunting for Godfrey and took over, grabbing him by the arm to make sure he didn't do a disappearing act. We hurried to the customer service centre and joined the queue. Someone shouted that the hotels were full. I remained steadfast. We were not going to spend the night huddled with our bags at the station. Godfrey seemed aloof, afloat in a sea of moving crowds and languages.

Someone called my name and I turned to see my friend Dorothy waving at me from the back of the line. We had been in the same dance group in Berlin for the past twenty-five years. I quickly motioned her to join us. We managed to get the last three single rooms at the Hotel Monopol, which I remembered as being quite close and reasonably priced, although we had already agreed that, for this evening, we wouldn't worry about money.

After we were safely checked in, we found ourselves in the hotel's old-fashioned restaurant sipping soup and wine. From our cosy table, we gazed open-mouthed through the huge window overlooking the street at the sight of trees bent almost horizontal in the wind and pedestrians struggling to move just a few steps and keep hold of their umbrellas and hats. None of us had ever witnessed a hurricane. It was like watching a film of a storm that had nothing to do with us. Next morning, after securing seats on the first train to Berlin, we learned of the devastation Niklas had caused. We had been very lucky.

We skipped breakfast to make the early train. Glad to be headed home, I thought back to our conversation the previous day. "Godfrey, your doctor made a connection between you teaching NVC and also experiencing war and saw them as being the same. I didn't quite get that."

He sipped a takeaway coffee, making a face; he would have preferred tea, but Deutsche Bahn was running with the bare minimum of services. No food either, which didn't bother Godfrey, he was like a camel and could go for hours without eating. "I see it as a connection between aggression and peace-making. I suppose I go out aggressively to make peace. The soldier analogy is just so right."

His gaze drifted out the window where we could see broken trees and shrubs, upended bins and other litter blown about by the hurricane.

"Did you notice you were closing your eyes while you were speaking?"

"A clever soldier never closes his eyes! A clever soldier keeps on looking behind as well, 'cos you never know where the danger's coming from!"

"Do you think you would really feel comfortable being a soldier, I mean like holding a gun. Doesn't that feel 'wrong' to you?"

By now, I knew that my friend loved speaking in military metaphors. After learning so much about his childhood, it was totally comprehensible to me; these were his earliest images.

"I still remember the horrible feeling I had when I once shot a heron. I was up in a tree and my father had trusted me to shoot pigeons – I was twelve – because they were ruining our crops. The heron fell to the ground. It was so big that I had to hold its feet above my head to carry it home. My parents were shocked that I had killed a sacred heron, but I had been up in that tree so long that I would have shot anything."

Godfrey's phone rang. It was a friend in Switzerland with news of an upcoming meeting ahead of a trip to Senegal. I knew he'd spent time in West Africa engaging in peace-work, NVC training and mediating and was curious to learn more about it. "What's it like?'

"Last November I visited The Gambia at the invitation of the UN High Commission for Refugees. They said about one thousand people had crossed the border from the Casamance region in southern Senegal, where there has been fighting between the separatist movement and the central government for decades. The refugees were escaping from the Senegalese police and military and UNHCR asked me to continue my mediation work and training with a group of about fifty of them. But someone in Paris, a member of the Senegalese diaspora who is a leader in the separatist movement and sees himself as the guardian of the region's honour, warned them not to attend my training, so only about twenty came. They were scared for their lives. I was scared even though I was staying in a guarded hotel."

"What motivates you to do this dangerous work?"

I couldn't really get my head around anyone's willingness to go voluntarily to a warzone, even if it was about helping to resolve a historic conflict. I wondered if I had been scarred by my parents' constant focus on The Troubles in Ireland. Why the hell did Godfrey dare to do this?

"I know when I go to some African countries that I am risking my life," he said evenly. "I go where the police or the army refuse to. I do it because it's important to support peace efforts and show people there are alternative ways of behaving instead of maintaining they are right and others are wrong. The last time I was invited it was to Niger, and my son, who manages Médecins Sans Frontières, advised me not to go. I didn't."

Six hours later we arrived in Berlin, hungry and ready for a late lunch at my favourite Italian restaurant in Charlottenburg, not far from the famous Ku'damm, an avenue of luxury shops and restaurants that cuts through the west of the city.

The next day, recovered from our adventure, I took Godfrey to visit my friends Dagmar and Ele, who had also been my dance instructor, at their cosy cottage on the banks of the Havel. After a long stroll along the river, we relaxed in the garden while my friends prepared a delicious barbecue. I played with their puppy Toni, who I regularly looked after. It was a lovely day.

Walking home, Godfrey said, "It looked to me like you and Toni were enjoying every second of your game, rolling around on the lawn, having fun. I said to Dagmar, 'Look at those two puppies playing!' There was a lot of love going on. Between you and them. You and the puppy. It was very sweet to see so much affection. Soothing and reassuring. It says a lot to me about the depths of your friendship that they came to pick us up. They don't let you down. Probably because you don't let them down. Up to that time I had thought of your caring for the dog as only a gift to Lorna, like you needing to have the affection, rather than it being a two-way thing. Today I saw something pretty unconditional."

"Unconditional love?"

"Yes, the love is there, no matter what happens during the relationship. There are no behaviours, accidents, no health problems that can fundamentally upset the relationship. It's the opposite of saying to the other person, 'If you don't behave in a certain way, the relationship will be finished.' I think unconditional love is something I get from you and something I would love to give back as well."

Although Godfrey's declaration tipped me a little outside my comfort zone, it warmed my heart. I felt a wave of affection for him. I resisted the temptation to shrug it off with a joke.

"Godfrey, you and I talked on one of our earlier trips about having an unconditional connection and agreed to reassure each other even if we lose touch. I love that when we sign off our e-mails, we just write LUCL [lots of unconditional love]. Even when you disappear or say things I don't like, it doesn't call into question the unconditional nature of the connection for me."

There, I had said it aloud and confirmed to him how strong our commitment was without showing too much emotion. British folk are weird sometimes.

Godfrey smiled at me. "I think unconditional love has played a very important part in my life. It is something I can see much more now I'm older. Like the unconditional love from both my parents when I was a child. Although my mother was very much into a God of retribution, a world of sin, punishment and reward, and my father was very angry, there was also a softness in both of them that suggested that anything could happen to me in my life and they would still be there for me. I find it quite moving to say that. And I think I can say the same of the relationships with my brothers and sisters; the undercurrent is unconditional love, that we are the Spencer family and everyone is loved no matter what they do. When our mother or father died for example, there was a sense of an unconditional bond."

I nodded, feeling a pang of sadness. I had spent many years imagining how different my life would have been if I had had a family like this. I sighed, and tried to bring my attention back to Godfrey as he continued:

"As I look at my life now, I think that NVC has played a huge role in maintaining a belief in unconditional love. Like the idea that human beings are only ever doing their best to meet their needs. There just is not a human need to harm anyone, even if that is the effect of our actions. There is something unconditional about that."

Godfrey paused and looked me straight in the eye. "When you said to me that our connection is unconditional, I knew what you meant. You are saying that you don't care about the incidents that happen in our lives, we will always be there for one another. I'm sensing that very powerfully during this implementation phase of our book project because I look to you as the person holding the energy. If you were not doing that, Lorna, this book would not be written. You give me two things: some sort of future, coming out of the present, and you give me a sense of trust that something will come of the efforts we are both making to bring this book to fruition and that's very important for me."

"I love that I can be cheeky with you and call you Bighead or Professor Earwig. You always laugh. How come?"

"Because there is intimacy in that, which I enjoy. I very much like the translation of the Italian expression for 'I love you': 'Ti voglio bene'. It means, 'I wish you well'. That for me is very much part of unconditional love. Just keep wishing each other well."

Our unconditional connection would eventually be put to the test. A little over a year later, our partners finally did meet when Ivan and I made a three-day visit to Saint-Étienne, where Godfrey, despite his expectations, was still living. He and Ivan got along really well, as I expected they would, and I liked Geneviève, who was a little shy about speaking English with us. Godfrey's simultaneous and swift translation helped our conversation flow.

One particularly hot afternoon, we sat in an air-conditioned cinema, with the place all to ourselves, watching Roald Dahl's children's story, The BFG (The Big Friendly Giant). Not only did we have fun with the main character's made-up language, Gobblefunk, the film also prompted a discussion about our childhood dreams, nightmares and friendships. In one particular scene, the BFG saves the orphan Sophie by asking her to close her eyes and jump, just trust that he would catch her. It seemed like a metaphor for life to me. We shared stories of blindly trusting and jumping into challenges and where that had led us. The movie was a real ice-breaker despite our differences and language restrictions.

And then, bidding farewell to Geneviève, once again I drove Godfrey to Montolieu for another EIC, this time with Ivan by my side. We departed in high spirits with plenty of time, deciding to take the scenic route through awesome natural parks, stopping for lunch at the charming medieval town of Figeac, a place I loved. I had looked forward to showing the south of France to Ivan, who was visiting for the first time. I have bitter-sweet memories of this trip. It was to be the last time I visited the Peace Factory and the last days I spent there with Klaus, another NVC trainer and something of a role model and father figure to me.

Klaus and I had never developed the kind of friendship I had with Godfrey, but every year, for the last decade, I made sure to attend a retreat at which he was teaching, in whichever country and in whatever language. I was in awe of him and his teaching skills. But it was his spirit that simply relaxed every fibre in my body.

I was delighted that Godfrey and Klaus invited me to join them on their early morning walks around Montolieu. Klaus warned: "It's not a stroll! It's a workout!"

Heading off at 6:00 a.m., we set a fast pace, walking for precisely one hour through the village and up into the hills, where, from the highest point, we could see the sparkle of what I took to be the Mediterranean and the start of the Pyrenees in the far distance, like a vast monument to nature on the horizon.

These dawn walks with two of the loveliest men I have ever met, were special, magic moments. Looking back, it was a glorious summer, full of laughter, joy, love and connection, dining, dancing, crying and singing together.

So, although I didn't see it coming, these times that I treasure would be the last Godfrey and I would spend together in person before an unexpected silence in our friendship that was to last eighteen months.

CHAPTER 13

OUR SILENCE

At the start of 2017, our friendship hit a bump in the road. I was caught by surprise. I had been working on our book, and had sent Godfrey a draft of the first three chapters. As we dialled into Skype, I was excited to hear his feedback.

"I can't read that," Godfrey stated. "The speech marks are incorrect."

I recoiled in shock. I had done a lot of work on these chapters and hadn't expected Godfrey to zero in on the punctuation mistakes generated by my German software. "Have you read any of it?"

"No. I've marked the pages with corrections though."

I was stung. "But what do you think of the content? All of that other stuff can be sorted out later."

He shrugged. My heart sank. I was desperate for some indication I was on the right track. I looked at his face on the screen, thinking, 'This is the ultimate test of our friendship and my commitment to this relationship.' Instead, I asked, "Can't you just overlook those bits and read the story?"

"No, I can't until the punctuation is perfect. I can only see the German quotation marks."

As we got to know each other, we had experienced many differences of opinion over the course of our friendship. We knew what made each other tick and where our passions lay. I was hurt by Godfrey's response – I had put in so much work already – and needed Godfrey to make a constructive contribution to the book, redistribute the weight. I felt insecure about the book and now, also, our friendship. Faced with either perfecting every grammatical and spelling error to meet Godfrey's standards before he participated, or the prospect of pushing forward on my own, our project ground to a halt. And so did our interaction.

Realising Godfrey would not, or could not, budge, I fumed inside. How dare he?

I was torn and upset.

Wallowing in disappointment, I felt my connection with Godfrey weaken. Negative thoughts swirled in my head about my friendship with him. I reflected on Irmtraud, another trainer at the retreat at Montolieu thinking we were a couple. I wondered if Godfrey had unintentionally encouraged her assumption over the years. I became quite unsure about our friendship. My priorities in life had changed. So had his. We were both investing time and energy into consolidating our relationships with our partners, and I was busy building up my consulting business. I learned later that Godfrey and Geneviève were busy planning to move in together and were searching for a new home in the mountains.

We drifted into silence, punctuated by the occasional e-mail. Then, in the autumn of 2018, our friend and inspirational colleague Klaus died after a ten-month battle with cancer. He had shared the news of his illness openly with the NVC community and as his condition had worsened, Godfrey and I rekindled our contact. Klaus was dear to both of us and we were concerned and sad.

At Klaus' funeral in Munich that cold November, Godfrey and I met again in person. Ivan and I collected him from the airport. He almost missed us as he hurried right past, but threw open his arms when he heard us call his name. There was no ice to break. We spent some very tender days at the lovely home of Gundi and Frank, sharing videos, photos and memories of Klaus. We joined about one hundred and fifty other friends and family in Tutzing near Munich to bid farewell to a man who had made an incredible contribution to the NVC community as a role model and trainer.

Looking back, Godfrey and I refer to this break as 'Our Silence'.

Preparing the manuscript for this book, I asked him: "Godfrey what do you think happened?"

"Lorna, I really am like a watering can with a hole in it. If I don't get my arse kicked, nothing happens!"

"Did you think about the book at all?"

"Oh, yes. I think I lost trust that it would ever come about. I thought I had let you down. And then I just got on with my life. I had no hard feelings towards you though!"

"Really? I imagined you cussing me under your breath. I had horrible thoughts about you. I was actually quite annoyed at your proof-reading. And behind my anger was a feeling of despair at how to take the next step."

"I felt terrible myself. I thought I had frightened you off. I am such a fusspot about punctuation. For me, the form reflects the content and I get so upset if I am ready to read and then I have to overlook mistakes. I didn't want to pressure you. I think it was another moment of masterly inactivity. I was disappointed with myself and went into hiding from you."

"And I went into hiding too, Godfrey. I was overwhelmed with how to complete the task on my own. It's funny how silence creates a pregnant pause and the mind fills it up with theories and reasons."

"I was meditating how impossible I am to work with. Maybe I had some accusation that you didn't do enough to bring me back. I had some fairly crazy inner dialogue, mostly about my inability to honour a relationship that you had called unconditional. I truly never had any bad feelings towards you, Lorna. I was trying to just love what is, as Byron Katie recommends, accepting the situation."

"There was something else that came up for me. I was a little worried that our friendship had become a bone of contention between you and Geneviève. I wasn't sure if she was jealous somehow."

"Not at all. She was convinced I would never manage to write a book and told me so. I think she felt disappointed with me. You know, Geneviève and I have known each other for years, but it wasn't until 2014 that our romance began and I instantly moved to Saint-Étienne to be near her. She had wanted us to sing together. I had shown interest in learning Tango with her too. None of that happened. She told me that I don't finish things, and she's right. I am not a finisher. I often start things, but someone else has to finish them."

That would have been helpful to know earlier. But I kept my lips buttoned as I had something more pressing to clear up.

"Another thing got me stuck, Godfrey, just after our last meeting about the book, I had a conversation with Irmtraud. And she expressed surprise at meeting Ivan at Montolieu. Until then she thought you and I were an item!" Godfrey laughed out loud. "Well, she had convinced herself somehow. After all, we arrived together at the Peace Factory, we left together, we were always chatting and giggling. And then after the incident with the participant who fell in love with you...."

"What? Who was that?" He seemed genuinely baffled.

"Oh, come on!"

We were back to our usual banter.

"You know what's weird Godfrey? It was Klaus who ended our silence. He got our friendship back on track."

Godfrey looked pensive.

On the screen, I showed him a picture of the three of us on a morning walk in Montolieu. Tears streamed down our cheeks.

"You got us back on track Lorna, you took the initiative."

In hindsight, I view our hiatus as part of our friendship journey, which has been rich in adventure and change. But I was glad to have Godfrey back in my life as a dear friend. I had so missed his stories and the laughs.

CHAPTER 14

"WHERE IN THE WORLD DO WE GO NEXT?"

Godfrey and I never did launch our joint training sessions, but we supported each other by brainstorming input, sharing learning materials and remaining good friends. My idea of being 'framily' had stuck. We didn't have to be in constant contact, but whoever reached out was always met with an unconditional presence by the other and a willingness to listen without judgement. And we still had fun pulling each other's legs, especially about our shortcomings in our relationships.

As we aired our complaints and grievances, one of us would chip in, "Well, it's better than a poke in the eye with a burnt stick!"

By the summer of 2020, around the world coronavirus turned normal life inside out and confined us to our homes. Godfrey had moved to the Pyrenees with Geneviève, and I was in still in Berlin, where restrictions after the first lockdown had almost disappeared. We spoke, as everyone had become accustomed to, over video-call. Even then, there was still a sense that the world would soon be back to normal. Godfrey was already planning to visit Germany in the summer of 2021 for an NVC International Intensive Training, in which I was also planning to take part. We were blissfully unaware of the tough times to come.

"How's it been moving in together in these strange times?" I asked him. Both Godfrey and I were used to our autonomy and space. Being stuck at home with another person had definitely been challenging for me.

"I still surprise her by not taking offence or worrying when she gets annoyed at me. It's simply 'masterly inactivity' on my part. I would have been a first-class student of Disraeli's."

I smiled. Referring to a nineteenth century British prime minister Benjamin Disraeli as a point of reference was so typical of Godfrey. I remembered from my history lessons that Disraeli had a reputation as a compelling speaker, who was very skilful at delegating detailed work to others.

"What about your NVC skills? Surely you use them with Geneviève?"

"If I try empathy, it riles her. I think she would like me to anticipate her needs, which I do try sometimes, like with the housework. I think that's very kind of me. Only I don't do unpacking, I'm very bad at that."

I laughed. I had had first-hand experience of this and was glad I wasn't involved this time.

Laptop in hand, Godfrey took me on a virtual tour of his new home. Showing me his expansive garden with its beautiful mature fruit trees and vegetable patch, he talked me through their plans to become totally food self-sufficient. I reflected on how the world had changed since we took our first car journey to Montolieu in 2012.

"Where are we, as in the human race, with climate change? Do you think we've made any progress?" I asked.

"I really lost hope when Donald Trump became US president, reversing legislation and pulling out of the Paris Climate Agreement. We've lost a lot of time. I don't know if these last four years are going to be just a hiccup in the timeline or if it's desperately bad."

"I wonder what Marshall would have thought about climate change? When he first came to Berlin in the nineties he didn't speak about social change, but that became a real theme in his later years. I'm convinced he would have been speaking about climate issues now."

Godfrey mulled this over as he walked inside and sat back down at his desk. I could see he still had his pyjama trousers on and smiled to myself, as I had just thrown a jumper over my night clothes. "I know that Marshall was very upset about a lot of things happening in society, but I don't think he ever lost the clarity that social change starts here and finishes here." Godfrey tapped a finger on his chest. "It's inside all of us. I don't like the idea of bossing people around so they take on our version of what we think they should be doing. If I bully people to change, I become a social-change terrorist."

"Movements like Fridays for Future and Extinction Rebellion, do you really think climate activists are bullies?"

I thought about the demonstrations in Berlin, some not far from my home, where activists had blocked a road and stopped traffic at a roundabout. The protests were creative, fun and exciting to watch. Godfrey smiled. He knew what I was referring to.

"Well, with the yellow vests [Gilets Jaunes] in France, I do think people got carried away, galloping forward hard on the bit, not really very conscious of what was going on around them. I like the idea of showing up, making a stand. But I also wonder about the pleasure people get, for instance, blocking a roundabout, and that has nothing to do with social change."

"I think of Marshall's concept of a 'giraffe scream', when you stand up to be counted, determined that your position be heard and taken in to account. When historically that has not been the case and for so long, like for people of colour or climate scientists, well, maybe that does justify a bit of bullying." I moved my fists toward the screen shadow boxing, trying to make a joke, but he only smiled wearily.

"That worries me. Bullying leads to violence, and if people lose their lives, you can't go back. A giraffe scream means simply stating your needs and requests clearly, with passion and a desire for change, but still remaining open to alternative strategies. If the feeling of anger is conveyed or your words include judgements, then your giraffe scream isn't one because it will imply that someone is wrong. And that won't get you anywhere."

"How do you think we can achieve social justice without some form of what you label bullying? You know, someone is always going to feel bullied and we don't have time to worry about that when it comes to the question of climate."

"When the cause is just and there is something that we can all agree to, like the Paris Climate Agreement, at least initially, and we know where we want to get to – use resources more efficiently, consume less – we have an option to live differently. History shows us that when you use violence to overturn a system, like the Russian or French Revolutions, then violence doesn't end."

"You mean changing the actors doesn't change the system?"

"That's it. All paths of change can lead to totalitarianism."

"I just don't see that happening. Greta Thunberg, a sixteen-year-old schoolgirl, can speak her mind with no regard for hierarchy – it doesn't wash with her – to the degree she tells world leaders gathered at the UN that they should be ashamed of themselves. Godfrey, it's because of her that I have decided to never fly again. I don't feel bullied into doing that, I'm inspired. And I'm talking to people about my choice and they are listening."

Godfrey took a deep breath. "I hear that you're not travelling by plane. I don't hear about you picketing the lines of the travellers at the airport and stopping them getting on planes. With a blocked roundabout, I do see bullying. People who have nothing to do with policy-making are blocked from moving forward."

"I am using my role as an elected delegate for the NVC trainers at DACH to put climate topics on the agenda. I haven't asked anyone's permission. When we last met in February, everyone present was happy to talk about climate change in relation to NVC and some 'came out' as members of the Extinction Rebellion movement. I might have been 'bullying' as you suggest, but from my point of view, I was bringing the needs of the planet into the NVC trainers' meeting because I feel no one else is bloody listening! And I am gonna keep expressing myself until I am heard."

"The danger I see is that you will end up believing that what you are expressing is right and that others are wrong."

"I do believe that I am right to draw people's attention to certain topics. Like equality in healthcare, climate change, social injustice. This last year has been like a huge wake-up call to humanity."

Godfrey listened intently, smiling and nodding, then closing his eyes as I continued calmly but determined. He was enjoying our debate.

"I believe I am right to speak up. I believe it is wrong to watch someone murdered in front of your eyes and not speak up."

I was thinking about the killing of a black man, George Floyd, in Minneapolis just a month before, when a white policeman knelt on his neck and he died after crying out that he couldn't breathe.

Godfrey seemed to catch my inference. "I agree with you there. In Saint-Étienne, Geneviève and I were walking down the street and saw a man throttling another man, who was turning purple. He couldn't breathe. I would have walked past. Geneviève, who is half my size, walked up to them directly and shouted, 'Stop!' Something shifted and several men in the gathering crowd moved forward to restrain the man. I do wish I had had the courage to say, 'Stop doing that!' and risk getting killed."

"That, to me, is not a case of her bullying anyone, if the intention is to save life!"

"That is frightening for me to hear because it can also be a license to kill."

"I don't agree Godfrey! I'm not killing you if I'm shouting, demonstrating peacefully but simply keen to be heard. I'm not killing you if I shout 'Stop flying!', 'Stop eating meat', 'Stop the injustice!'."

"I like that. But am still worried about where your success could lead you. It would be better if we were able to curb our passions and do things *for* other people rather than *against* them."

"In German there's a word, 'Selbstläufer', which means actions assume a life of their own and create an automatic dynamic of change."

"That's it!"

"When I watched the video of George Floyd, I asked myself why was no one stopping those policemen from killing him?"

Given the hurt, anger and injustice surrounding Mr Floyd's death, I might have felt uncomfortable discussing the details of his murder, but not with Godfrey. I was sure he would understand my questions without judging me.

"They would have got shot. And there were so many policemen not visible in the film."

"That's the conclusion I came to as well. Standing back, or filming, was probably the safest thing the onlookers could do. I do get it, but I would have had survivor guilt after that."

I continued: "Here's my question: What is it that can create a willingness and ability to step up and get involved, even if we are risking our lives? Maybe I need training in bystander intervention like the Hollaback! teams offer. I've just learned about their work; so inspiring! I do ask myself, as a white woman, am I willing to go up to a white man and shout, 'Get your knee off that man's neck!' Am I too afraid of the uniforms, as if they're magic costumes? You know, with my Irish hot-headedness, I might just have gone in there and taken the risk. I don't know!"

I paused. Godfrey smiled. I knew he believed I might have just done that.

I shook my head. "You know, I've never lived in a more frightening time."

"Lorna, I'm glad we're frightened, that generates energy."

We looked at each other on the screen. I had come to treasure the ease with which Godfrey and I could slip into a conversation about anything and explore even the most difficult topics together.

"Maybe, we've had our last car journey together, Godfrey, should we take the train from now on, like we did from Frankfurt?"

Godfrey winced at the memory of Hurricane Niklas.

"If I could be persuaded that trains are more ecological…" He sighed and shook his head. "It's just occurred to me how much we were polluting the atmosphere driving through all those countries. I'm quite shaken by the thought."

"Maybe then in future, you just stay put in the Pyrenees and I stay here and we'll Zoom."

"Do you know how polluting Zoom is? When Google set up shop in Belgium, they built their offices over a marsh. And their consumption of water was enormous because the servers get so hot. Is that what we want?"

"We can't go back to caves and drums. Tell me, what would your perfect world look like?"

"It would be a place where a critical mass of people has already moved from self-affirmation to compassion. I believe that the future of humanity lies there. If we continue simply to affirm what is, we will continue to be competitive, we will continue to destroy. And if we could get to a place where I, me and you, matter, where there is no social or racial injustice and all living things matter, that would be a place I would dream of living in. At the moment we have so many people in the world who only move forward at the expense of others. Some very successful business people, who have expanded their businesses, their wealth, are still carrying the belief that they can go on like that forever. They can't, if we are all going to go on. We have to work collectively, with an acute sense of 'us' and 'we'. I would love to see a place where we can be, with dialogues, where everybody feels safe all the time."

I sighed. "Maybe that's utopian."

"Yes, it is. And I don't mind that."

"I remember something Marshall said, 'Get very clear about the kind of world you would like and then start living that way'. I remember an outing after the EIC at Montolieu to nearby Carcassonne. The narrow streets were packed with tourists admiring the beautiful stone turrets and crenelations. Remembering an image from Asterix and Obelix, I joked that our group should keep in tortoise formation, like a Roman army advancing protected by shields over their heads and to their sides. Klaus smiled at me and said, 'No, we go in with open hearts, see them all as human beings. We'll all be fine.'"

"Yay! That's a place you can drive me to." Godfrey threw back his head in a full, throaty laugh.

"I was really impressed by an email I received from another NVC trainer, Robert, asking all NVC trainers to consider being vegetarian." I watched for Godfrey's reaction. "He spoke of his own choices and said it makes sense to him that, as teachers of NVC, we don't eat meat. He said he was astounded by how many trainers do."

"Did he give you the impression that he wanted you to buy his ideas?"

"Not at all. He wrote, 'Please, if anything of this mail resonates with you negatively, if you have questions, if there is something that you feel is judging you or your choices in any way, please let me know and when you do, tell me which bit triggered you, and how it triggered you'.

He was precise, not taking any responsibility for triggering an emotion in others, instead asking for a dialogue. It was a welcome wake-up call, beautifully and respectfully put about his pain, his sharing, and totally on eye-level. That would be the style of communication I would like to see in the world I would like to live in."

"I'll go there with you. Take the wheel! I think that my dream is also of a place where I would be much more aware of my demands in respect of other people. I notice often I am still in 'demand mode' and not tolerant of others' points of view, treating people in a way I would not like to be treated myself. Part of my dream then is to walk my talk better."

It impressed me, as always, that Godfrey willingly questioned his integrity and could express self-critical reflection. It was a rare quality that warmed my heart.

"What would make it easier?" I asked.

"A very quick inner check to recognise that the needs I have that the person in front of me isn't meeting, are met in other parts of my life. That eliminates the urgency to get a particular person to meet those needs for me."

"That wouldn't help me. I would be getting on my high horse with thoughts like, 'You can't behave like that!' Sometimes, it's hard to remember that I'm actually scared when I'm angry. I would need a place where it's okay to be scared and it matters to someone if I'm feeling like that, like a Ministry of Anxiety. Anything you're scared about, you just call them up and there is someone to empathically connect to you and take into account what it is that scares you. Does this sound mad?"

I felt a little out on a limb with this idea.

"You'd like to know that if you are scared you could get support? Like when someone has headaches, we point them in the direction of medicine to help their healing?"

I nodded. Then added: "Maybe we don't have to go anywhere."

Godfrey began to sing: "'There is a place where you can always go' … Marshall sang that many times at the end of his trainings. 'Stay right where you are. Where it's all right to let your feelings show'. We've already got that place; I think we are actually there already!"

I understood what he meant: the communities, retreats and groups we had experienced where folk were adhering to the principles of NVC that Marshall had taught and shared. That community was growing by the day, embracing the passion to express feelings and connect to needs as a universal life energy.

Godfrey continued: "You know when I think about the last fifteen years and how our friendship has evolved, I am quite moved. It would be quite natural for people to think we indeed had some form of romantic intimacy; it is quite unusual for two people of the opposite sex to have such a deep friendship over so long a time, especially with a generation gap of twenty-five years."

I was astonished this was the first time the idea had crossed Godfrey's mind. I feigned shock, and then grinned. "Well, you do know that some people have speculated...?"

His laughter boomed through my screen.

"Godfrey, for me, that is the special thing with you, that despite us being different in gender and age, having very different life experiences, we do indeed have a very special friendship, without any form of physical intimacy. Someone suggested we may have been siblings in a former life. I just thought of the way we pick on each other and still have fun."

Godfrey beamed at me. I knew he was remembering his fondness for his older sister, Sabina. Was this what it might have been like to share the stress of my childhood with a loving sibling?

We fell silent for a few minutes and just stared at our images on the screen. I could see Godfrey's eyes fill up and glisten. He coughed softly and then sang a line of one of his favourite songs, his usual party piece at the end of a retreat. "All is well, I'm safe and sound, all is well, there is peace upon my river homeward bound."

We had been chatting for an hour and my timer pinged. It was time to go.

Godfrey put his hands together as in prayer and nodded, smiling with his eyes closed.

"So, Godfrey, we'll meet again soon. In this world or the next, as the Irish say. LUCL to you my dear friend."

And, as the screen closed, I saw our faces, briefly frozen in time. And then we were gone, until the next time.

EPILOGUE

What a rollercoaster our years of friendship have been. What started as a means to calm a jumpy passenger – encouraging Godfrey to reminisce about his extraordinary life as I drove him across Europe – has evolved into a book about our personal connection.

Looking back, we both treasure the bubble of intimacy we created in my little Citroen. Our conversations meandered, took unexpected turns, entered new territory and re-trod old paths, travelling back and forth in time, to different countries, places, people, describing our life experiences and childhoods. Godfrey's memory never fails to amaze me. Driving time flew by.

I don't deny there were one or two instances when I felt the urge to drop him at the next intersection with a sign around his neck, just like Paddington Bear, stating his next destination and a note to "Please look after this gentleman". My heartstrings twang as I write that. I do wish for my friend, who despite the challenges in his life, of war, violence, loneliness and loss, and truly is a gentle man, to be looked after.

Sharing similarities and differences of our life events created a bond between us. A friendship to cherish. Completing the editing of this book, chatting over video call from our homes in Berlin and the Pyrenees while cases of Covid-19 soared again in Germany and France, has been another step in our friendship journey. In the long process of preparing the manuscript, we have quibbled, procrastinated, changed our minds and debated, particularly about the concepts and practices of Nonviolent Communication, our understanding of which differed considerably sometimes. My use of colloquial, contemporary language in NVC settings infuriated Godfrey, triggering his worry of diluting the core, the spirit of what we both hold dear. Having both survived childhood trauma, we share a passion in our hearts to see all children safe and well, nurtured and thriving, but we hold very different perspectives on parenting and parental support systems. Through very honest discussions on ethical issues, especially in our educational roles, such as the question of intimacy between teachers and students, we have confronted sensitive, topical issues around power and consent in relationships. Discussions of boundaries, selfcare and conscious decision-making fuelled our itinerary, as we discovered historical landmarks, exquisite landscapes, some excellent European cuisine and shared hearty laughter. And all the while, our lives changed in sometimes challenging ways, with new relationships, homes and work opportunities.

When we began our travels almost ten years ago with that first drive to Montolieu, I was chuffed that Godfrey, my teacher, asked me for a ride to the retreat. Today, we are allies, confidantes and trusted companions through the ups and downs in life. I still love listening to his stories and am astonished that he still has so many I haven't heard before. Occasionally he'll mention a recollection that I have written about here and I am fascinated that he will recount it almost word for word. I have read every story many times over. I am surprised how little he bores me. I look forward to our calls and I often think of him, funnily enough mostly on Sundays. It was on a Sunday, after a long period of estrangement from my mother following my arrival in Berlin, that I used to have a weekly phone call with her in the years before she died. I envisage him in his lovely garden, drinking tea with Geneviève (or hot water, her favourite), looking up at the Pyrenees, occasionally jumping up out of his chair because he has remembered something he had forgotten to do.

Godfrey has definitely become framily to me. What a delight it has been to listen to him share so much of his rich life experience. And our story is not over yet.

THERE IS A PLACE

By Cinde Borup and Beth Pederson

There is a place, where you can always go - come with me.
Where it's alright to let your feelings show - come with me.

What a pleasant journey, isn't very far,
We can go together, stay right where you are.
And now it's time to start,
It's right here in your heart.

There is a place where you can be yourself - come with me.
And it's a place where you can free yourself - come with me.

And you know it's waiting, not so far away,
Need no reservations, we could go today,
Now it's time to start,
It's right here in your heart.

And the light shines through each window,
And the door is open wide,
And each question has an answer
If you'll only look inside.

There is a place where every sorrow ends - come with me.
Where every hope and every truth begins - come with me.

What a pleasant journey, isn't very far,
We could go together, stay right where you are.
Now it's time to start,
It's right here in your heart.

And now it's time to start,
It's right here in your heart.

Lyrics to "All is Well" and "There is a Place" (Cinde Borup, Copyright 1994) published with kind permission of Beth Pederson. High Noon Music: 1019 Ruth Ave, Sandpoint, ID 83864, USA, +1 208-263-8706, www.highmoonmusic.com.

ACKNOWLEDGEMENTS

From Lorna:

Ultimately this book would never have been possible without Marshall Rosenberg, and I will always be grateful to my friend Andrea Fritsch for asking me to attend my first workshop with him. Gratitude too to all we have mentioned in various chapters, companions along the way, and those who supported us by proofreading first drafts, such as Honor Mary Dolan. There are many more who have supported me personally, especially: Frank Heibert for keeping me dancing, Claudia Broadhurst for encouragement, Dawn Reeves for sharing her publishing experience and honest feedback, Claire Darwent for being a great pal, Marilyn Tresias for being a guardian angel when she was most needed, Christa Klema and Margret Bäuerle for being my framily, our hosts Aileen and Fred, Clarissa, Virginia and Matthew, to Klaus Karstädt for his immense contribution to my life and generosity of spirit, Louise Romain for organising the EICs, everyone I encountered within CNVC and D-A-CH e.V. who have shaped my understanding of NVC and expanded my knowledge, and Bert for his everlasting friendship (although I know he will never read this). Most of all I thank Victoria Robson for her invaluable experience and gentle guidance as our editor, and of course, Ivan J. Barry who was the first to read every word, share comments and encouragement, and who listened patiently to every idea, thought, emotion, and brought me endless cups of tea.

From Godfrey:

My heartfelt thanks to my previous employers the North Atlantic Treaty Organisation, IBM, and of course, the inspirational Marshall Bertram Rosenberg, the originator of Nonviolent Communication, an art of living that has shaped my life exponentially.

Thank you also to my family and friends. In large and small ways, you have all helped me to become the person who I am - myself.

And most profound gratitude and thanks to Lorna, who encouraged me, travelled with me, cajoled me to relax, to open up and lift the lid on my maze of memories. Without her, I could not have opened my heart and revealed myself not only to her, but also to me and now, dear reader, to you, in the form of this book.

RESOURCES

Godfrey Spencer: https://thepositivecommunicationbusiness.com
Lorna Ritchie: www.lornaritchie.com; www.lornaritchie.de

Nonviolent Communicationsm **Organisations and Networks**
www.cnvc.org (international)

https://nvctraining.com

https://dach.gfk-info.de (German-speaking countries)
http://trainer-gewaltfreie-kommunikation.de
https://www.fachverband-gfk.org

https://cnvfrance.fr/ (France)
https://cnvbelgique.be (French-speaking Belgium)
https://nvc-uk.com (UK)

Other sites we discovered and loved whilst writing this:
https://www.ihollaback.org/about/
https://peerspirit.com